ACT OF ATONEMENT

Also by John Bishop

ACT OF MURDER

ACT OF DECEPTION

ACT OF REVENGE

ACT OF NEGLIGENCE

ACT OF FATE

ACT OF ATONEMENT

A DOC BRADY MYSTERY

John Bishop, MD

MANTID PRESS

Act of Atonement

A Doc Brady Mystery

Copyright © 2022 by John Bishop. All rights reserved.
ISBN: 979-8-9861596-2-1 (paperback)
ISBN: 979-8-9861596-3-8 (eBook)
ISBN: 979-8-9861596-4-5 (hardback)
Published by Mantid Press

For information about this title, contact:
Attention: Permissions Department
legalquestions@codedenver.com

CONTENTS

CHAPTER 1

PREACHER AND BULL

Sometime in the early 1970s

The day began with such promise. Two friends, and very unlikely ones at that, making a trip south and east just to eat at Kitty's Purple Cow in Surfside Beach, Texas. Kitty's had the best burgers in those parts—double meat, double cheese, with bacon and jalapeños, served on a toasted sesame-seed bun slathered with butter and Kitty's own brand of homemade aioli sauce. You could sit outside at a redwood or concrete table under a palm-thatch umbrella and enjoy the sounds of the beach near the confluence of the Gulf of Mexico and Galveston Bay. Or so Bull had said, since he was the experienced diner at Kitty's.

As far as Preacher could recall, Bull had no other name. Of course, Bull had a first and last name, but Preacher couldn't remember what they were and really didn't care. Preacher had so few friends in his crazy, mixed-up life, he was happy as a clam just to have Bull as his traveling buddy.

Bull and Preacher were hobos. The word "hobo" sometimes had a negative connotation, implying "bum" or "tramp" or just about any word that would describe someone who didn't work and more likely than not was also a "wino." But Bull and Preacher took great offense at being called any one of these other names because, in their respective minds, a hobo was simply a traveling worker. A bum did not work at all. A tramp worked only when forced to. But a hobo, well, he was gainfully employed but didn't have enough money or social skills to have his own transportation, and definitely did not fit into one of the molds you're supposed to fit into to be a so-called "normal" member of the work force.

Preacher and Bull liked their wine, there was no denying that. Thunderbird, Night Train, Wild Irish Rose, all favorites. These wines were "fortified" and, through some process of fermentation that they didn't understand, ended up being around 20 percent alcohol. This amount of alcohol packed a wallop, both while you were drinking it, and most certainly when the morning hangover arrived, accompanied by the sledgehammer that pounded your head until the cure arrived, which was more fortified wine. An endless cycle, for sure, but that was their life. Not that they would turn down beer or cheap whiskey, but wine seemed to be the cheapest and most accessible alcohol available, and certainly had the most predictable outcome.

The other fact of their respective lives that embodied nonconformity was their mode of transportation: riding the rails. That, in train lingo, was the epitome of being a hobo, at least in the mind of the railroad employees, who spent many a dollar trying to rid the freight trains of the scourge. Although there were many trains to choose from, Bull and Preacher loved the Katy, short for the Missouri-Kansas-Texas Railroad Company. Say M-K-T a bunch of times in succession, and you get Katy for short. The Katy's tracks ran from Kansas City all the way to Galveston, Texas.

The Katy was the most liberal in allowing "traveling workers" to board their freight trains without paying. Of course, the tricky part was running alongside the tracks, grabbing a ladder that was welded to each boxcar, and hoisting yourself up without getting run over by the rail wheels. Bull and Preacher had seen their share of men literally cut in half while trying to board a train illegally; it happened when getting off the train, too, although it was much less common.

The Katy used "yard bulls," essentially railroad cops, to police the train stations and railroad yards. Their job was to secure the railyards and prevent theft from or damage to railroad property. So, men who were riding the rails were on constant lookout for the bulls, whose job was to keep the boxcars clear of hobos and the like. But you couldn't watch everybody all the time, and usually, eventually, men like Preacher and Bull were able to board a train illegally and head out for their destination.

This was how Preacher and Bull met. Bull was himself a yard bull based in Oklahoma City, a Katy terminal. And Preacher lived in Oklahoma City, that is, when he was sober and had gainful employment. Preacher's skills ran along the line of sales. He had worked for many door-to-door sales companies, including Fuller Brush, Encyclopedia Britannica, and Sunbeam Vacuum Cleaners. But his specialty was selling the New King James Bible. Man, he could sell those Bibles. Problem for Preacher was that selling anything involved cold calling on households, and back in those days, for the most part, the men went to work, the kids went to school, and the wives stayed home alone. And with his good looks, that afforded all sorts of opportunities to get himself into trouble.

Bull, back in the days of his employment with M-K-T Railroad, had thrown Preacher out of an empty boxcar so many times, he couldn't remember. Over time, they would have conversations about life (which were usually enhanced by fortified wine). They struck up an odd friendship and started traveling together. Bull was able to maintain his job as a railroad bull via a special dispensation from the Katy bosses, so he was able to ply his trade in the various cities along the Katy routes—Kansas City, St. Louis, Oklahoma City, Dallas, Fort Worth, all the way south to Houston and Galveston. And Preacher did whatever Preacher did to eke out a living.

And so it was, on that warm night in July, that Preacher and Bull deboarded the Katy in Galveston, Texas, and by some small miracle were able to hitch a ride in the back of a pickup the forty miles to

Kitty's Purple Cow just before closing time. Preacher had a bottle of Night Train left over from the ride down from Oklahoma City, and while Bull ordered their burgers, Preacher staked out an outside table and listened to the surf.

Bull brought out a tray stacked with the burgers, fries, onion rings, and two tall glasses of iced tea. While they enjoyed their meal, and took their time eating, they noticed a good-looking young woman, one of the few remaining customers, giving Preacher the "eye." Or at least Bull assumed she was looking at Preacher. After all, Bull was over six feet tall, heavy, and nearly bald, and he had a mug on him with all sorts of distortions from multiple fights. Preacher, on the other hand, was five feet eight inches or so and a lean 140 pounds, with a full head of black slicked-back hair and a smile that showed his pearly whites in all their glory. And the more the young woman stared, the madder Bull became.

Preacher tried to defuse the situation, having been in this position before, but to no avail. Bull had killed most of the bottle of wine by himself, and he wasn't a pleasant drunk. All of a sudden Bull stood up, yelled something to the effect that he was sick and tired of Preacher having all the fun, and pulled out a pistol. It looked to Preacher to be a .25 caliber, which was a peashooter, but a gun was a gun and capable of killing when aimed at the proper body part.

Preacher stood and tried to wrestle the weapon away, meanwhile hearing screams from the folks eating their dinner and trying to clear a getaway path to safety. The two struggled, and with Bull being the much larger man, he was able to gain dominance with the gun. But it seemed to Preacher that maybe the wine had weakened his friend, and suddenly he felt he was gaining control of the situation, when the weapon discharged. There was silence for a moment, and then Bull began to fall. Blood began to stain Bull's chest. Preacher felt the weapon slip from his friend's hand, and Preacher used that moment to look around his torso to make sure he wasn't the one that was hit. No, clearly Bull had taken the round and was falling fast.

Preacher screamed for help and tried to use napkins to stem the flow of blood from what was now an obvious entry wound in Bull's chest. All he could hear in the background was "call the police" and "there's been a shooting" and "there's a murderer at Kitty's." As Bull fell, Preacher fell with him, and he saw the light beginning to leave his friend's eyes. Bull wasn't going to make it, and there Preacher was, holding a gun, and about to be the obvious choice of whom to blame. Fear took over, and he lit out.

CHAPTER 2

NURSE RITA WALKER

Tuesday, September 3, 2002

My mother, Lucille Brady née Peck, had a younger brother by the name of Howard Peck. Seemed that Uncle Howard found himself in a bit of medical trouble, or so she told me on the phone the previous evening. He had been admitted to University Hospital in Houston, Texas, for a liver transplant.

She knew, of course, that I was an orthopedic surgeon at that same institution, and she had called to ask me for a small favor. Knowing my mother as I did, there was no small favor one could do for Lucille Brady. I won't say that Mother was demanding, controlling, and possessed of an ego that would be befitting of one of the Gaelic royals, but she was a piece of work. She often said if she were chief executive of these United States, she would fix all our international issues in one day. I'm sure that would have involved the keys to the various nuclear arsenals, but fortunately for us ordinary citizens, Lucille Brady would not ever assume that role. That venom came from a woman that was five foot two inches and shrinking, with flaming red hair and a tongue whose sharpness could cut a rib eye steak as easily as a Miyabi knife could. My mother obviously did not adhere to that old saying, "Be sure and taste your words before you spit them out."

As a result of our conversation yesterday, I found myself at the nurses' station on the eighth floor of the University Hospital's Medical Division, Transplant Unit. It was just before 3 p.m. on Tuesday, which we docs all know to be the "shift change" time. Most nursing personnel work one of three shifts: 7 a.m. to 3 p.m., 3 p.m. to 11 p.m., or 11 p.m. to 7 a.m. Some of the staff are able to work twelve-hour shifts, three days per week, but they are in the minority. The reason I came at shift change was that there was so much going on involving the transfer of patient information during that time that the nurses got a little distracted from noticing doctors that may or may not have belonged in a particular area of the hospital, such that I would have had a better opportunity to review Uncle Howard's chart even though I was not on the transplant team. With all those HIPAA privacy laws, the patient's hospital chart had become more like the Holy Grail, such that the nursing staff guarded the chart with aggression.

"Afternoon, folks, Dr. Jim Brady here. How's everyone?"

"Just peachy, Doc. Shift change, so you know how that is," answered an attractive woman who seemed to answer for the remainder of the staff present, which I would estimate at fifteen or so.

They all stared at me as though I were an alien. I had on my gray scrubs and a white coat with my name engraved, so it was obvious that I belonged there. Maybe not in this particular unit, but at least in the hospital.

"What can we do for you?" asked the woman that seemed to be in charge, whose name tag read Rita Walker. She was tall, had light-brown skin, and wore her hair in a short Afro. "I haven't seen you before. Are you new staff?"

"No ma'am, I'm an orthopedic surgeon and spend most of time in the University Orthopedic Hospital sector. I'm here to try and get some information about a patient."

"Which patient?" she asked.

"Howard Peck. He's scheduled for a liver transplant."

"We know Mr. Peck very well. Have you been called in for a consultation? I don't think we have any orders for an orthopedic consult, do we?" she asked in the general direction of one of the staff members sitting at the massive semicircular built-in desk that ran from one end of the nursing station to the other.

"Not that I know of, at least from the day shift," the ward clerk answered.

"Sorry to confuse you. I'm not here in an official capacity. Howard Peck is my uncle, my mother's only brother, and she asked me, as a favor, to stop by and see him."

Nurse Rita looked at her staff, all murmuring amongst themselves, nodding their heads as if they knew a secret and I wasn't in on it. "I see. Guess you want to take a look at the chart, see if we transplant folks up here are doing our jobs?"

"Not at all. I thought I would just familiarize myself with his problems, such that if he asks me some questions about his medical condition, I wouldn't appear to be a complete dumbass."

This comment changed the atmosphere, with the staff generally smiling, laughing, and nodding heads.

"Get me the chart, Cindy," said Nurse Rita. "Come on, Doc, we have a nice cubicle where you can review Mr. Peck's chart in private and smarten yourself up."

Uncle Howard's chart was about the size of the Gutenberg Bible. It would take me way past cocktail hour to review it all. I looked for a summary of some sort as I pulled out my cell phone and called Mary Louise, my bride of thirty-one years.

"Hey, big boy," she answered. "Want to come up and see me sometime?"

I started to close the chart and head home.

"Before you storm out of there, Jim Bob, have you seen your Uncle Howard?"

I sighed. "I have the chart in hand and am about to review it. It's unbelievably thick. It will take me forever," I whined.

"You promised your mother you would check on him and get back with her. So please stay there and get that off your to-do list. I'll have a nice cocktail for you when you get home. I made you your favorite, pot roast with new potatoes."

That did not encourage me to stay on the floor and do chart review. "Fine," I said. "See you in a while."

"By the way, Fran called me this afternoon, said a lawyer had called your office, wanted to speak to you."

"Oh God, not a lawsuit, I hope."

"Apparently not. He told Fran it was personal. I'm just relaying the message. Fran says you have a problem with cleaning off your desk and she wanted to make sure you returned the man's call, so she gave me his information."

"In my experience, any call from a lawyer is a bad call."

"Don't get distracted. Finish up there and come home to me. Hugs and kisses. See you soon."

Uncle Howard, according to his sister, my mother Lucille, was the favored one of my mother's kin in his younger days, voted amongst the family "most likely to succeed." He was just too good-looking for his own good. Wavy black hair, black eyes, a ladies' man, so to speak, and a cross between Rudolph Valentino and Count Dracula. He also had the gift of gab and was a smooth talker from his childhood days. The family party line was that Howard was a traveling salesman of sorts, when he wasn't at home nursing a bad back. The story in the family was that Howard had inherited a spine problem that wasn't correctable surgically. He worked for a number of different companies but was an unreliable employee due to his frequent absences from work. He predominantly sold Bibles, the perfect job for an on-and-off worker, or so Mom told me.

Truth of the matter, however, was that back in the day, Howard was a drunk. A fall-down, slap-happy drunk. He rode the rails—train speak for "he was a hobo." He went from place to place, sold Bibles, made a few bucks, then went on a bender. From time to time he would get lonely, or broke, or sick, and would go home to his wife and family, or call one of his seven sisters and ask for help. My mother was no exception, and she would be called on from time to time to help out her wayward brother. I can remember as a kid, hearing the phone ring after my mandatory bedtime, sounds of my parents arguing, and my dad using Howard's name in vain, expletives deleted. Eventually, I would fall back asleep, awaken for breakfast and school, go into the small kitchen, and see my uncle at the table. Back then he was a handsome man and very friendly and outgoing. He would get up from his chair, give me a big hug, and ask about my life in general. I was a little afraid, him being the only hobo I knew, but at the same time, he was quite the charmer.

This scenario happened a few times during my childhood and adolescence. And then at some point, he never came calling again, at least as far as I heard. I asked Mother about it a time or two, and she would say that Howard got sober and had been called to be a preacher in East Texas. And that if I found the time, he would be at the next Peck family reunion and she was sure he would love to see me. The good news was that I had become involved in sports back when I was a teen, and since then, I'd had an excuse for almost every day in the summer, which kept me from enjoying a Peck family reunion. Attending college and becoming a doctor had successfully kept me away since then. The last one I remember, we were in the Sam Houston National Forest, camped out in a smelly canvas tent, in the rain, and my crotch was on fire. I later determined a wood tick had found a new home in my pubic hair and was partying down there all weekend. I had to get a knife and carve the damn thing out once I returned to civilization, no small feat for a fourteen-year-old kid. That was my last reunion visit, after which I adopted this philosophy: "roughing it" meant no room service.

These memories of my childhood ran through my thoughts as I reviewed Howard Peck's hospital chart. He had cirrhosis of the liver, which comes from a lot of drinking. A couple of bottles of booze a day for over twenty years should do it. He had presented to the emergency room in Zavalla, a small town in East Texas in the area where I assumed he lived. He had turned yellow—jaundice in medical terms—and had almost scratched his skin off. That's called pruritis, and it comes from a buildup of toxins in the bloodstream once the liver can no longer metabolize these chemicals properly. As soon as the docs over there took a look at his blood chemistries, he was transferred to the University Hospital System in Houston.

A complicating factor was that during the workup by the oncology service here, he had been found to have a cancer of the liver as well, confirmed by CT (computed tomography) scan, MRI (magnetic resonance imaging) scan, PET (positron emission tomography) scan, and a careful biopsy. It occurred to me that Howard was essentially a goner, so how could he have possibly qualified for a liver transplant with cirrhosis AND cancer? I needed to read more and do some medical research, but my stomach was growling, and I really wanted my cocktail that Mary Louise was going to have ready for me. Besides, I knew enough to go and say hello to my dear old uncle, and I could answer some general questions if he had any. Plus, I could always provide the ultimate disclaimer: I'm an orthopedic surgeon, and as far as I know, there are no bones in the liver. A lame answer, but it worked for me.

Nurse Rita Walker appeared in my cubicle with what looked like a cup of coffee.

"Thought you might need this. It's black, so if you need cream and or sugar, let me know. I just figured a man wearing cowboy boots probably took his caffeine straight up."

"You are so kind. Thanks much. I admit I was starting to sway, reading all this medical data. Gives me a headache."

I took a sip. "The coffee is strong, just what I needed, and much better than the swill that passes for coffee in the doctor's lounge in the orthopedic hospital."

"We bring it in from the outside and brew it fresh several times a day. Anything else you need? I'm the three-to-eleven supervisor, so I'll be around for a while."

"I'm good. You've been very kind. I have to go in and see my uncle now. His prognosis looks pretty bleak, wouldn't you say?"

"Yes sir, I would. Dr. Robert Damon is the oncologist in charge of his care and had a meeting yesterday with the hepatologist, the radiologist, and the transplant surgeon. Seems that the mitigating factor in his treatment is the discovery of the cancer in the liver. Normally that would contraindicate a transplant because in most cases the cancer has spread to other organs before it's diagnosed. In your uncle's case, the tests all show that there has been no spread. That in itself is a small miracle. So, the doctors agreed that without evidence of spread, the transplant is a go. It's on for 7 a.m. tomorrow. Dr. Ed Crawford is scheduled to do the actual procedure. He's about the best there is."

"Oh, I remember Dr. Crawford from medical school and internship. He's a magician in the operating room. First time I ever met him I got called to scrub in on a case with him, something in the abdomen in a grossly overweight patient. He already had three assistants in there holding retractors and still couldn't see his way to find the gall bladder. He had taken a break, waiting for me, his fourth assistant. He came back to the operating room and shoved the door open, with a lit cigarette hanging out of his mouth. I thought the anesthesiologist was going to have a stroke. He started yelling at Dr. Crawford about how it wasn't his day to get blown up and he better put that damn thing out and get back in there before the patient coded. At the time, it was pretty frightening for me, a novice, but as I continued through the next five years of orthopedic training, that episode ended up being one of the highlights. We didn't get blown up, as you can see."

"Dr. C. finally gave up those Picayune cigarettes, and it just about killed him. But he's still going strong. Well, I've got to get about my business. It was nice to meet you. Let me know if I can help with anything. Your uncle has a long road to recovery ahead of him."

"You've been great. I appreciate it. You have a wonderful smile, by the way, that puts patients at ease, I'm sure. It certainly worked on me."

She laughed, we shook hands, and I headed to Room 802.

CHAPTER 3

UNCLE HOWARD

Tuesday, September 3, 2002

"**L**ong time no see, Uncle Howard," I said, shaking his hand. "Mom asked me to come by and check on you, not that you need my help. You have the best doctors in the world here on the transplant team. They will take excellent care of you. I understand your surgery is tomorrow."

"Yes, Jim Bob, and I thank you so much for stopping by. I haven't seen you in years. You know, you quit coming to the Peck family reunions quite some time ago, so none of the family has really kept in touch with you. It's nice to see you have turned out to be a handsome man and a prominent surgeon. Looks like all the doting your mother did ended up being a worthwhile endeavor. Good thing she was persistent in seeing that you followed her advice and went into the medical field."

That comment started burning a hole in my gut, since I essentially put myself through college and medical school and did it ON MY OWN. But since he was having a liver transplant in the morning, I thought I should let my better angels take over and show a little kindness toward my parents.

"Yes sir, don't know what I would have done without Lucille Brady watching over me. So, I looked over your chart, and I see that you have both cirrhosis and liver cancer. I remember, from when I was a kid, that you used to drink pretty heavily. Or at least the few times I saw you, you were in need of help, shall we say?"

"That's right, and although I got right with the Lord many years ago and became a teetotaler, old Satan still had his way with me, and my liver has just rotted away."

"Well, I'm not sure how much Satan had to do with it. Liver failure is—"

"Oh yes, Jim Bob, Satan had his way with me all those years ago. Kept me on the bottle. I hate to think about all those wasted years, drunk and riding the rails all over the Katy lines. Lucky I didn't die sooner of some other disease, considering my lifestyle."

"How old are you now?"

"Just turned seventy-two, and I sure would like to see seventy-three. You know, Jim, one of the reasons I wanted to talk to you was about the cost of all this. We're not people of means."

He looked about ninety-four, but I didn't say that to him. His hair was gone for the most part, except for a few wispy strands over the ears. His skin had a yellow tinge from the excess bilirubin in his blood, but it was a pasty color of the sick and dying. He was propped up on a few pillows and had an oxygen canula in his nostrils.

"Well, the good thing is that you're on Medicare now. That will offset the cost a great deal. It's pretty expensive to have a liver transplant—well, any transplant, for that matter. All the doctor bills, hospital charges, the procedure itself, plus the long-term care, what with the anti-rejection medications, probably will total close to a million dollars. But once you have the transplant, you go onto Medicaid, which really helps with the cost of all the meds. I think you need to concentrate on getting through the surgery tomorrow and the subsequent treatment. I think that right now, the cost is the least of your problems."

"Jim Bob, I believe the Lord works in mysterious ways, His wonders to perform. You know I became a Methodist preacher, don't you?"

"I remember something about that, yes."

"Well, I've been preaching God's Word for most of my life, and preaching God's Word sober for over twenty-five years now, and I've done most everything possible to atone for my past behavior. And that's another reason I asked your mother Lucille to have you stop by and visit. I'd like you to do something for me, in case the surgery doesn't turn out well and I go home to meet Jesus tomorrow. I didn't want my wife to hear this conversation, so I sent her and my son down the hall to visit with my older son, the liver donor."

"Your son is your donor? I just assumed you were on the transplant list, and your number came up, so to speak."

"Both my boys have turned out to be fine men. Ron has followed my footsteps into the ministry, and Rico has his own pawn shop and jewelry store. Rico is a perfect match, so he's donating a portion of his liver to save my life."

"Ron and Rico? Sounds like a rum drink to me."

He laughed. "Yes, a little humor from the old days. My wife didn't like it, but she understood. By the way, the surgeon told me not to worry about Rico donating part of his liver. Said something about that it grows back? Is that right?"

"Yes. The liver is the only organ we have that can regenerate itself, so he'll be fine in six to twelve months. Pretty amazing stuff, huh? Anyway, this favor?"

"Back in my drinking days, I killed a man—my best friend, in fact. I want to make amends for my actions."

And he began to tell me the story of Preacher and Bull.

CHAPTER 4

MARY LOUISE

Tuesday, September 3, 2002

"**S**o, how are you, and how was your Uncle Howard?" asked Mary Louise, as I entered our high-rise apartment on the twenty-seventh floor of the Post Oak Tower.

It never ceased to thrill me to see the Houston city lights from this height, as well as the enormous array of cars traversing Highway 59 and the 610 Loop. Ah, the joy of the south-facing view.

"As promised," Mary Louise said, as she handed me what appeared to be a very cold dirty martini. For the last two summers, I've switched from Macallan scotch to martinis.

I sipped, put my empty arm around her waist, gave her a hug, and received a chaste kiss on the lips. "I am so much better now. Thanks. You smell good. How are you feeling today?"

Tip, our golden retriever, nuzzled his nose between us and gave me one of his many baleful looks, as if he wondered if he would be left at the kennel for another month, or worse, returned to the farm of the patient who had given him to me as a gift after a successful surgery.

A year and a half ago, Mary Louise was involved in a horrendous traffic accident. Another vehicle T-boned her Jeep at a high rate of speed. She sustained multiple fractures of her upper and lower extremities and had a head injury that kept her in a coma for several weeks. I was distraught beyond description after her injury, couldn't work, couldn't take care of Tip, could only sit by Mary Louise's bedside and wait. I was certain Tip remembered his absence from our lives and seemed to be constantly worried that those circumstances were somehow his fault. He had been an exceptionally good boy since our family reunited. He was grateful, but still seemed a little sad.

"Better today—I didn't use the cane!" said Mary Louise. "I even stayed awake during a March of Dimes board meeting that ran past schedule, then survived a late lunch at Carrabba's. I may smell fresh as a daisy but I certainly don't feel like one. The board wore me out today. Anyway, tell me all about Howard and his troubles."

I rendered the events of the day with Uncle Howard and Nurse Walker, sipped my martini, and watched Mary Louise complete my favorite dish of pot roast and vegetables. "That was some story he told me. I can't even believe it's all true. I mean, how could he remember all that detail? He was drunk most of the time, according to family legend."

"Poor man. He's probably been through hell, keeping those events bottled up all these years. Did he say how he managed to get back to Galveston after the shooting? It sounds like he was on foot, and with the police obviously looking for him, it's a wonder he wasn't arrested and jailed at the time."

"True that. Well, it was night, and it's basically flat bayou country between Surfside Beach and Galveston, with lots of sea grasses for camouflage. I don't know how he did it, but he managed to walk those forty miles without being caught, then caught a boxcar on the Katy and got back to Oklahoma City. He said that was the last day he ever touched alcohol. He went back to school, became a Methodist minister, and the rest is history."

"And he was how old?"

"He said around forty."

"What a story. You certainly have some interesting relatives."

"Tell me about it."

"By the way, do you want some red wine with dinner? I opened a nice Chianti just in case."

"Yes please. Have I told you today that I love you?" I inquired.

She had this strange look on her face as she limped around the kitchen counter and gave me another kiss, this one with the promise of things to come . . .

"I don't want to hurt—"

"Shush," she said.

We eventually had to reheat the pot roast . . . no big deal. It was especially tasty.

"So, what about this murder?" Mary Louise asked, once we'd turned in for the night. "What in the world can you possibly do at this point in time? That was what, nearly thirty years ago? And what about the authorities? How can you possibly look into this without informing the police?"

"No idea. I thought I would call up J. J. and see if he might be able to help me out. Uncle Howard never discussed the murder with anyone, not even his wife or his sons. I can't just call up the police department in Surfside and ask about an unsolved murder from thirty years ago."

J. J., our son and only child, had a private investigation firm he had established, with his college roommate Brad Broussard as partner, called B&B Investigations. I thought of him more as Philip Marlowe or Sam Spade with a smart phone, but I rarely verbalized that. They handled all sorts of inquiries and did work for private corporations, governmental agencies, even the Houston Police Department.

The HPD was still run by my old friend and patient Chief Stan Lombardo, although it did appear that his daughter, and Mary Louise's best friend, Detective Susan Beeson, had advanced through all sorts of obstacles to become the front runner to replace her father. She and I had been through a few battles together, ferreting out the evildoers in the medical and nursing professions. She was a top-notch detective and would be a fine addition to the Houston police hierarchy.

"I'll give J. J. a buzz tomorrow. I'm beat. I've got a busy day in surgery tomorrow, and I can barely keep my eyes open."

"Me too. Short evening at home but very nice, young man."

"Sadly, I'm not that young anymore. You make me feel younger than I am, and for that, m'lady, I am very grateful."

"What about the lawyer you're supposed to call? And do you want me to take Tip down for his—?"

I gave her a pat, rolled over, and was gone.

CHAPTER 5

ORTHOPEDIC SERVICE

Wednesday, September 4, 2002

I was what was called an academic orthopedic surgeon. What that meant in plain English was that I devoted a certain amount of my work time to teaching. In exchange for teaching, I received a salary from University Medical Center. And in response to that salary, the institution gently and quietly plucked half of my income for "overhead expense." My CPA told me that the university was getting the far better deal, and that I was generously donating about 25 percent of the moneys I could have been taking home back into the system. But it was difficult to complain about my work situation, and I didn't see how I could have had any better job, even if I somehow took my practice elsewhere and retrieved that extra 25 percent of income. For the time being, I continued to ponder the situation. I was good at that. Pondering.

Mostly I taught residents and fellows. Residents were those individuals that had completed medical school and a year of internship and were on a four-year track to complete their orthopedic training program. Fellows had completed those years of training and were Board Eligible or Board Certified, depending on whether or not they had passed the Board Certifying Exam in Orthopedic Surgery. Fellows could in fact have been in practice, working for a living. However, they desired further training in a particular area of orthopedic surgery, which, in my case, was hip and knee joint replacement, and that extra training involved another year of working under a specialist's tutelage.

So it was that I arrived at University Hospital at 5:45 a.m. for rounds with the fellow, Dr. Tim Stacy, and the resident, Dr. Shelley Compton, who was rotating through my service to learn what she could about hip and knee replacement.

Young Dr. Stacy was thirty-three years old, married with three children, and owed a mountain of debt. I mean, four years of college, four years of medical school, five years of internship and residency, and then a one-year fellowship? That was fourteen years of higher education. And factoring in that he had been getting paid only a subsistence salary for the previous six years, how could he not have been in massive debt? Considering the cost of housing, food and clothing for a wife and three children, and the amount of debt accumulated over the course of the training program, it was a miracle that any sane person wanted to undertake that sort of task.

Dr. Compton was a little better off. She was married to an ophthalmology resident. She had no children yet and had, from what I understood, a wealthy family who was subsidizing her and her husband's expenses during their respective training programs. Shelley was a small woman, about five foot three inches in height, and couldn't weigh more than 105 pounds. She was fit and ran marathons in her spare time—not that there was any—and had good tensile strength but wasn't a bulky, muscular individual, which you would think would be necessary to install hip and knee replacements. Shelley was leaning, I thought, toward doing a fellowship in hand surgery, but when we were in the OR, she could manipulate the leg and pound those prostheses in just as efficiently as Tim could.

Tim was a big guy, six foot six inches or so, probably 250 pounds, and was an All-American tight end for Rice University. He never wanted to go pro; he always wanted to follow in his father's and brother's footsteps and go into the "family business," which was orthopedic surgery. The Stacy Orthopedic Clinic was located across town on the southwest side of Houston and enjoyed a reputation of providing excellent orthopedic care to their patients.

We three met as usual at the nurses' station on the eighth floor of University Orthopedic Hospital, along with the head nurse for the 11 to 7 a.m. shift, Gracie Johnson.

"How goes it, gang?" I asked.

"All your patients are stable, Doc Brady," Gracie responded. "Got a couple of folks that need to give up their beds here on this floor today if they want to get their bill paid. They're both pretty slow on the physical therapy, but I believe that they could go to rehab for a week or two prior to home care. These insurance people are getting really nasty about moving patients out of their hospital beds on a pre-ordained schedule and either sending them home or to another facility. To me, it's all about the insurance companies lowering their costs, and to hell with the patients' welfare."

"Gracie, you have the problem figured out. Now if you could just come up with a solution that the doctors, nurses, hospitals, and insurance companies would all agree on, I believe you'd win the Nobel Peace Prize. Until then, we need to get rounds done."

"Hey, Doc Brady, before we start, I got to share this with you."

"Tim, this isn't one of your bad jokes, is it?"

"No sir, I got this from my buddy doing an OB-GYN residency. It's the gospel truth."

I saw both Shelley and Gracie rolling their eyes.

"So," Tim continued, "you know how the government has gone wild with all these HIPAA rules about patient privacy? Well, my buddy said it's so bad that when he's at clinic with one of the private docs, and the nurse opens the door to the waiting room, she is no longer allowed to call out the patient's name. So, to cooperate with the government and avoid a fine for violating HIPAA rules, the doc has instructed the nurse to simply announce to those in the waiting area, 'Will the patient with the leaky bladder please come in.'"

Rounds finally done and breakfast eaten, I headed back to my area in the University Orthopedic operating facility. I used ORs 36 and 37 all day Mondays and Wednesdays. I dedicated Tuesdays and Thursdays to patient care in the clinic. For almost twenty years, I tried to operate in the morning and see clinic patients in the afternoon, but I was always late. With the changed—I called it upgraded—schedule, it seemed I was mostly on time and certainly less stressed out. If some sort of emergency arose, it could be added to the schedule without causing a riot in clinic.

We had four cases to do: a "virgin" hip replacement, a "redo" hip replacement, and two "virgin" knee replacements. There was a big difference in virgin joint-replacement work versus redo joint-replacement work. Most of the time, implants lasted ten to thirty years. Sometimes they did not. And when an implant had to be replaced, all that cement, along with the prostheses, had to be removed with care so as not to fracture either the tibia (shin bone) or femur (thigh bone). That took much more time than just implanting a prosthesis for the first time.

We finished all four cases by 2 p.m. For logistical reasons, I put Tim in the room with the redo surgeries, since he'd had the most experience and those cases were the most difficult, and Shelley in the virgin prosthesis room. They both were good assistants and were capable, when the procedures were completed, of washing out the wounds, sewing up the tissue and skin, and applying the dressing. That allowed me to go back and forth between the two operating rooms, which shortened the operating time and the anesthesia time.

It was a good system for patients and staff alike and was a routine procedure for most of the busy surgeons at University Hospital.

I dictated my operative reports, went out and talked to the families, and headed up to my office in University Towers.

CHAPTER 6

FRANNIE

Wednesday, September 4, 2002

"How was your day, Pop?" asked Fran Makowski, my secretary for twenty years, having held that position nearly as long as I had been in practice. She had a way of standing in the doorway of my office, one hand on her hip, looking like she knew something I didn't. She was skinny as a rail, but about five feet nine inches, with longish brown hair. She could be imposing when she wanted.

"Fine. What is it?"

"Whatever do you mean?"

"Fran, after all these years, we know each other pretty well. We can read each other's moods, almost say what the other is thinking. You've got a little bee in your bonnet. What gives?"

"Your mother called today. Six or seven times."

"What in the world for?"

"About your uncle, her brother. Seems his transplant was delayed."

"Did you find out why?"

"Well, I called the transplant unit, then Dr. Crawford's office. They had an emergency that bumped your uncle."

I quietly seethed. My mother could be such a colossal pain in the butt. You can't really blame the surgeon. An emergency is an emergency.

"How did you leave it with her?"

"I told her what I just found out, and she finally quit calling. His surgery is supposed to start about 4 p.m. if you want to get in on the action."

"Fran, that's just what I need after four joint replacements. To go over and stand around like a fifth wheel during a highly charged organ transplant procedure. Plus, look at all this paperwork on my desk. I can't even see tomorrow's schedule," I whined.

"That paperwork will take you ten minutes. You need to go over there so I can tell sweet Lucille Brady that I was able to get you to do what she wanted you to do."

And there it was, coming out in all its glory, me doing what Mom wanted. If only Dad were still alive, God rest his suffering soul. He was the only person who could set her straight.

Unfortunately, Dad developed pancreatic cancer at seventy-five, and declined treatment. True, he had seen several of his friends turn up with that disease and had seen them undergo the "curative" procedure, known as a Whipple procedure. Basically, it's a procedure where the surgeon goes into your abdomen and cleans everything out. That's not exactly accurate but close enough. Not one single friend of his had survived, although some lived for twelve to eighteen months while throwing up their toenails every day due to the required postoperative chemotherapy.

Dad finally went peacefully in his sleep, aided by the morphine drip installed and monitored by the angelic nurses from hospice care. Such pain he had endured until practically the end, when he finally got partial relief with the medication. I pondered why we wait so long to end the suffering of our loved ones and patients from a terminal disease. I swear, we treat animals better than people.

"Where's Rae?" She had been my nurse for almost sixteen years.

"She had to take one of her grandkids to the doctor. She just now left. Don't worry, I've got everything under control," said Fran, as she handed me a slip of paper with a name and number on it.

"Ah yes, if only other surgeons had a secretary like you to run their business. It would be a life-altering experience for them. What's this?"

"Administrative assistant, Pop."

"Huh?"

"My title is administrative assistant, and that's the name and number of the lawyer you need to call."

"That probably means you do the same job you did when you were called a secretary, just at a higher pay rate, right?"

She winked at me. "Better git to gittin', Pop. Don't want your mama mad at you. Call the lawyer; that might change your life."

And with that, she shut my door. I swear I heard her snickering in the hallway. And what was that about changing my life?

The University Hospital System was a massive array of office buildings and hospitals. It covered two or three city blocks in the University Medical Center. With the Houston weather being hot and humid most of the year, the architects were smart to design a series of walkways on the second level, connecting all the structures over Main and Fannin Streets. We docs never had to get out in the elements to see patients, nor did families have to endure Houston's weather to visit patients, for that matter. The walkways were all open to the general public, after of course paying a week's wages for a parking spot.

It took me half an hour to get over to the transplant unit of University Hospital. By then it was almost 4 p.m., and I was happy to see that my new acquaintance Nurse Rita Walker was on duty.

"Dr. Brady. What a nice surprise to see you. Are you here to see Mr. Peck?"

"Yes ma'am. My office staff told me his procedure had been delayed."

"That's right. Dr. Crawford had a dissecting aortic aneurysm come in, and that bumped Mr. Peck's transplant to later in the day. Then there were some complications with a post-op transplant from yesterday and Dr. Crawford had to take that patient back to OR to stop the bleeding. He's had a long day, but now it's your uncle's turn. In fact, the orderlies wheeled him and his son, the donor, over to OR about a half hour ago, so they should just about be ready."

"Okay, Rita. Thanks much. Sounds like Dr. Crawford has a job that wouldn't suit me very well. Early in my training I thought I wanted to be a heart surgeon, but after two months on the cardiovascular service, and not being able to go home during the rotation, I decided I wanted a life beyond work."

"I don't blame you, Doctor. Not one bit. Good luck to your uncle. He's a good soul, in my opinion."

CHAPTER 7

DEATH

Wednesday, September 4, 2002

I made my way over to the operating rooms of the transplant service and introduced myself to the charge nurse. That's doctor-speak for the head honcho. I told her about wanting to check on my uncle, Howard Peck. She suggested I go up to the observation deck above OR 12, that it should be empty this time of day, and that I wouldn't have to put on a "space suit" to see the procedure. The operating room attire for heart transplants was similar to what we used in orthopedic surgery, the goal being to do everything possible to avoid an infection during the procedure. The space-suit system consisted of a helmet with a battery-operated fan, a unique gown made of a special fabric that does not wet with water or blood, and a special visor that allowed the surgeon to see clearly while preventing sweat droplets from contaminating the wound. Add to all that a room equipped with laminar air flow, and you had a modern-day operating environment.

Since I had just spent the last six hours suited up doing my own cases, I opted to climb the stairs inside the operating suite and watch my uncle's liver transplant from the observation deck. We didn't have one of these in the orthopedic surgery sector. There were two in this wing of University Hospital, one for transplant observation and the other for cardiovascular surgery observation. These were considered high-end specialties that attracted many visiting surgeons to Houston to observe current procedures and technologies.

I was astounded at how clear the operating field was through the plexiglass roof of the OR. I was only six feet above the operating table. That particular observation room held fifteen seated observers. The chairs were quite comfortable, but hopefully not such that attendees would fall asleep during the transplant.

After 5 p.m., I was usually ready to ditch my scrubs and change my environment, as in drink a cocktail, munch on appetizers, and sit down to a nice dinner with Mary Louise. It was already 4 p.m., and in my mind the clock was ticking.

Uncle Howard was under anesthesia, and his abdomen was already open. There were towels inside the belly to keep the tissues moist, and the operating staff appeared to be waiting on the donor liver-transplant organ. Normally there were two teams, one to harvest the donor organ, the other to transplant the organ into the recipient.

About that time, Dr. Crawford burst into the room. The circulating nurse removed his gown and hood and replaced it with sterile space-suit components, and he started to work. He deftly clamped the supporting vessels around the diseased liver and slowly cut away the existing tissue, removed the organ, and set it aside. Almost simultaneously, another gowned-and-gloved staff member entered the OR with a covered stainless-steel pan and handed it to the scrub nurse. She removed the towel and presented the donor organ to Dr. Crawford. It didn't look like much, just a reddish-brown piece of organ with stubs of blood vessels and tissue ducts attached. He began stitching the donor organ to the recipient's supporting tissue. He glanced up at me and told the circulating nurse to turn on the intercom.

"Brady, is that you up there in the observation deck?"

"Yes sir, Dr. Crawford. I'm just here to observe how the real surgeons work. That happens to be my uncle there."

"Well your uncle has about the worst-looking liver I've ever seen. The damage from the cirrhosis is bad enough, but the extra disease from the cancer? I told Damon the oncologist that I have my doubts as to whether this is going to work. I would hate to be wasting a perfectly good piece of liver from—who is it? His son?

"Yes sir. I don't know enough about the physiology to even have an opinion. Just going along with what the experts recommended."

"How long has it been since you were on my service?"

"Oh man, maybe thirty years."

"And now you're a bone doc here?"

"Yes sir."

"Well, I might want to talk to you about this damn hip of mine. I'm up to twelve ibuprofen a day and I can't sleep on that side."

"Sounds like 'old Arthur' to me."

"You mean arthritis?"

"Yes sir."

"Well, if I ever get a break from the OR I'll come get an x-ray."

"Happy to help, Dr. Crawford."

He was somehow able to expertly sew the liver to the supporting vessels while talking, then started looking around for any residual bleeding after the vascular clamps were removed. It looked to me like he was satisfied with what he saw, but then—

"What the hell? Suck down in the hole. I can't see where that blood is coming from," he yelled to his surgical assistants.

The assistants, one on each side of the table, started using the suction machine to stem the welling up of blood, but in spite of their efforts, blood continued to rise up in the wound.

"Pressure's down, heart rate is up. We're going to lose him if you don't get that bleeding stopped," said the anesthesiologist.

"Don't you think I know that!" thundered Dr. Crawford.

He continued to siphon large amounts of blood from the wound, but to no avail. There was a major vessel that had ruptured, or some stitching had come loose, or my uncle's blood was refusing to clot due to liver damage, but there was so much blood, Dr. Crawford couldn't see well enough to determine the problem. The staff called a code, and shortly there were four more docs in the OR, trying different meds to get the blood to clot, and trying to elevate the blood pressure to save the patient's life. They instituted open-heart massage, a last resort in a code blue, but since the abdomen was already open, it was a short reach into the chest cavity.

This went on for another thirty minutes, but to no avail.

My uncle, Howard Peck, was dead.

CHAPTER 8

LELA BELLE PECK

Wednesday, September 4, 2002

I called Mary Louise from the crosswalk on the way back to my office and the parking garage and told her the bad news. As it turned out, she gave me news that wasn't much better: my mother had come into town for the surgery and was waiting at our apartment to hear all about it. I decided that it would be prudent for me to go back to the surgical waiting room, seek out my aunt and the cousin who wasn't the donor of liver tissue, and at least make my presence known to them and assist with any instructions from the treating surgeon and his staff.

The problem was that I hadn't seen either one of them in years, so recognizing them would be an issue. As I walked into the waiting room, I saw Dr. Crawford and his nurse talking with an older woman and a man somewhat younger than me. I presumed those were my relatives, and I strolled over. I had never been good with death and dying, which was why I chose orthopedic surgery. Folks were injured and fixable in my field, and rarely did I have to deal with autopsies and grieving families.

"We're not sure what happened, Mrs. Peck," Dr. Crawford said. "All went well with the transplant. The anastomoses were pristine when we completed the hookup, but then he started to bleed uncontrollably. We did everything we could do, but nothing worked. I'm sorry, but he's gone. We need to get your permission for an autopsy to find out the cause of your husband's demise. It won't help him, but it might save another life down the road. That's no consolation to you, I realize, but it will provide valuable information for the future of liver-transplant surgery."

He patted her on the shoulder, and he and his nurse walked away.

"It's been a long time, but I'm Jim Bob Brady, your nephew. I observed the surgery on Uncle Howard. So sorry for your loss. Is there anything I can do?"

She gave me a huge hug and sobbed. She appeared to be about my mother's age, was very short, and had gray hair.

"I know who you are, silly. It's been years . . . too many years. Howard always loved you and was so proud. You remember Ron, don't you? My other son?"

No, I didn't, but I shook hands with him as though I did. Ron was a good-looking man, taller than his mother, my aunt, with a full head of fair hair tamed with gel.

"I don't know what the procedure is now," I said, "but I'll get with the nursing staff and administrative personnel and let them take it from here. Where are you staying?"

"Next door at the Marriott. It's attached by a walkway above ground."

"Yes, I know. It's a great convenience for patients and their families. Well, I'm headed home shortly. My mother is there. Do you and Ron want to come over, get something to eat?"

"Thanks so much for the invitation, but I think Ron and I will grieve to ourselves tonight. Maybe some time tomorrow we'll see Lucille, but I just don't think . . ."

"I totally understand. My mother is not the best in these situations, is she?"

"That's an understatement. We'll talk tomorrow, okay?"

"Of course." I gave her another hug, shook Ron's hand again, and went to the admissions desk to initiate the process of removing the body and whatever else was involved after a death. And then I realized that since I hadn't seen my aunt before the surgery—Uncle Howard had sent her and Ron down to see Rico, the donor son, during my visit so my uncle could tell me about the alleged killing he committed years ago—that I could not for the life of me remember her first name.

"What do you mean, Howard is dead? He's at the best institution for a liver transplant in the world, and he doesn't make it through the surgery? How is that even possible?"

My mother grilled me like it was me personally that did her brother in. I went through all the information that I had at my disposal and explained that hopefully the autopsy would reveal the secrets of death that his doctors could not see at the moment.

"Well, that won't bring him back, will it?"

"No, ma'am, it won't. Sorry I can't tell you anything else, but that's all I have."

"Huh. Some doctor you are," she said, as she stormed out of the kitchen into the guest bedroom, where I hoped she wouldn't stay for too many days.

My mother was the oldest of eight or nine children, and although she rarely spoke of it, I had deduced that she had lost most of her own childhood taking care of her younger siblings. Her anger, dissatisfaction, and resentment had spilled over into her adult life, making her a chronically unhappy woman.

"Well, that went well," I said to Mary Louise.

"How about a martini?" she asked.

"Maybe two? What are the dinner plans?"

"I ordered in from Carrabba's—penne and tagliarini pasta, Caesar salad—your favorites. I hope your mother likes Italian food."

"At this point, I can't say that I care. Do you have any idea what Howard's wife's name is? I'm drawing a blank."

"Lela. Lela Belle, actually. How was she?"

"Well, one thing is for sure. I invited her over for dinner and to visit with Mother. She declined. Said essentially she wasn't in the mood for Lucille Brady, reading between the lines."

"Well, then she can't be all bad, huh?"

I laughed. "Frannie reminded me to call that lawyer, said it might change my life. Any idea what she meant by that?"

"All she told me was that it was a personal issue, and considering your aversion to attorneys, we both thought it would take the two of us to convince you to make the call."

"Do you still have the number?"

"Of course. Why don't you have your drink and make the call while I heat up dinner. Frannie said this was his cell number, not an office number, so that seems to be a good sign, wouldn't you think?"

"To quote old Billy Shakespeare, 'The first thing we do, let's kill all the lawyers.' That's the only good lawyer sign I know of." I sipped and dialed.

"Tom O'Leary."

"Mr. O'Leary, this is Dr. Jim Brady. You called me?"

"Yes sir, thanks much for returning the call. I have a personal matter to discuss with you. When's a convenient time?"

"You said a 'personal matter.' What do you mean, exactly?"

"I'd rather discuss it in person. There are some sensitive issues involved."

I thought of all sorts of sensitive personal issues: paternity suits, sexually transmitted diseases, bankruptcy, income tax evasion, the heartbreak of psoriasis . . .

"What sort of sensitive issues, sir?"

"Let's discuss it in person. Friday, day after tomorrow, looks good for me. How about you?"

I didn't have anything rigid scheduled for Friday. I normally would make rounds, clean off my desk, and unless an emergency surgery came in, Mary Louise and I would head to Galveston late morning.

"I could do 10 a.m. Friday morning. Is my office all right?"

"Of course. I have your address. Hopefully I can find it amongst the maze of buildings there in the medical center. That complex makes driving around downtown Houston look simple. See you Friday, Dr. Brady."

Tip had "the look," so I put the remains of my drink into a to-go cup and we headed to the lobby. I sensed some urgency on Tip's part and was glad the powers that be at Post Oak Tower had invested in high-speed elevators. I leashed my boy as the doors opened, greeted the night security man, and walked through the sliding doors out onto the green grass reserved for dogs off to the east side of the property. Tip looked at me in relief as he squatted. I swear he smiled.

CHAPTER 9

SARA

Thursday, September 5, 2002

I was up early on Thursday as usual. I passed my mother's room on the way to the kitchen and coffee pot. Her door was closed, so I decided to leave it that way. No need to poke a hornet's nest or step on a fire-ant hill without provocation, was my motto.

Tip was sleeping in with his mistress and was glad to have her home. He had raised his head when I arose, sniffed at Mary Louise, and returned to slumber. I envied him.

I made rounds with the usual crew of Tim, Shelley, and Nurse Gracie. The post-ops from the day before were doing well and expertly pressing the buttons on their respective morphine pumps with regularity. Some of the other patients were on the launching pad for discharge, either to their place of residence or to a rehab unit of some sort. Overall, no problems were noted.

I had a bite to eat in the surgeons' lounge and headed up to clinic, which began at 7 a.m. I looked over the schedule and noticed a large red star at 3 p.m., with no one scheduled after that time. I asked Fran and Rae what that was about.

"Special patient," they said in unison.

"Oh man, not another Tamborinian royal. I'm starting to suspect they have more royals than standard citizens in that country."

"Of course. They just l-o-v-e Dr. Brady."

"Bodyguards again? And do we have to clear the clinic of all other patients? And both the University Hospital president and the Chief of University Orthopedic Group show up to greet members of the royal family?"

"You got it, smart boy," said Rae, while Fran did her snickering routine.

It's the inequity of patient care, the haves and have-nots that irritated me so. Some patients could barely put food on the table, while the Tamborinians flew around the world in private jets. Their money was from oil and gas production in their tiny eastern European country, handed down thru the royal family chain of command.

I would have no problem having Dr. Greg Mayfield stop by. Greg was probably my best friend. We had gone to medical school together, as well as internship and residency. We were separated for a year by fellowships, mine in hip and knee replacement, his in spinal surgery, then we both returned to the University Orthopedic Group and had been partners for over twenty years. Greg was much more of a politician than I, which had allowed him to rise up the corporate ladder to chief of the University Orthopedic Group.

The president and CEO of the parent institution, University Hospital, was Dr. Ben Silverman. Ben started out as an internal medicine/hematology specialist. He had elevated himself through the ranks of the medical hierarchy, partly on his own merit as a tremendous academic physician and teacher, and partly due to his father's gift of $50 million to build the Silverman wing in University Hospital. Ben and I got along fine, but because of my small-town and humble beginnings, I was always a little intimidated by a member of the silver-spoon crowd.

By 3 p.m., the clinic waiting room was a ghost town. Both Ben and Greg made an appearance prior to my examination of my new patient. I sat in my office and dictated charts until the mucky mucks had completed their greetings and the patient entered my clinic area with her entourage. This procedure had become routine for me, even the two bodyguards carrying Uzis, of all things.

I entered the exam room, which was made crowded by the patient, who was in a full-length traditional embroidered Tamborinian caftan, as was the custom for traveling Tamborinian royalty; a man I assumed to be the husband, similarly attired; and another woman, said to be the translator. The two bodyguards wanted to be in the exam room as well, according to my nurse, Rae, but there just wasn't enough room. I put my foot down and said no, knowing that, in spite of the visual threat, I had no reason to be expecting to be filled with automatic weapon fire on the spot. Fortunately, the translator agreed with me, and she and the patient's husband shooed the bodyguards into the hallway.

The translator introduced herself. "Doctor Brady, I am Nabila. I am serving as translator this afternoon. I believe we have met before?"

"I think so, Nabila. How are you today?"

"Fine, sir. This is your patient. She is Her Royal Highness Princess Sara of Tamborinia. And this is her husband, His Royal Highness Erik, Prince of Tamborinia."

I made a gesture to shake the man's hand, something I had momentarily forgotten one was not supposed to do with royals, because he recoiled like I had thrown a rattlesnake at him. Remembering myself, I nodded at my patient and she nodded back. "And this is my nurse, Rae, whom you've already met." Rae knew enough to cut straight to the nod.

Examining a patient in a heavy full-length caftan is a challenge. Especially when the husband is present in the exam room, and especially when the problem involves the hip. To examine a hip, one must hold the leg by the foot and ankle, rotate the hip, and flex and extend the knee, all of which requires manual manipulation. In other words, touching the patient. In this case, the royal patient. And because the husband continually tried to shoo my hands off his wife's leg, I was unable to perform the examination properly.

I had seen and operated on all sorts of royal clientele, from couples in stunning upscale dress with three-piece Brioni suits for the men and Chanel dresses for the women, to very conservative couples like the one in the exam room that day. And maybe I had become jaded over the years, but if I couldn't examine the patient, then I wasn't going to treat the patient.

I told Erik, "Sir, I have to examine your wife. She has a hip problem, or at least I was told that's why she is here."

"You are not to touch my wife. That is the law in our country."

"Well, sir, this is Houston, Texas, and if you want me to treat her, I have to know what the problem is. And to do that, I must examine her. And to do *that*, I need to be able to touch her and I need her to be in a hospital gown."

"You may take X-rays, or scan. No touching."

With that comment, Sara turned to her husband.

"Erik, get out. The doctor needs to examine me. Go play with your sheep or something."

Erik hung his head and left the room.

"Sorry about that, Dr. Brady. He can be such an ass." She spoke to me in perfect English. The King's English, that is, not Texas English. "I'll put on the gown if you'll step out, please."

After she changed, I completed the exam, and it was obvious she had a very painful hip during all planes of movement.

"How long has the pain been bad?"

"Two years. I fell off my horse three years ago. The doctor at home said it wasn't broken, but it never quit hurting. It got better for a while, then the pain returned. He was an idiot, I think."

"We'll get an X-ray and talk some more."

Rae escorted the patient to the X-ray department. The husband followed along, with his head bowed.

"Sorry about that," Nabila, the translator, said. "It's a chronic problem with the royal men that come from Tamborinia. They want to play by the same rules as they do at home, and it just doesn't work. As you can see, Sara is the major royalty, and Erik is only a fringe royal. He tries to pretend he's in charge, but then Sara will, how do you say in English, 'drop the hammer?'"

"Funny. That's probably from a Clint Eastwood or Bruce Willis movie."

"I'm sure, Doctor."

I went and got a cup of coffee while waiting on the X-ray. The Uzi duo had accompanied Sara and her husband to X-ray, again on the lookout for miscreants in the waiting room.

Sara returned, and the technician hung the films up on the view boxes in the exam room. Erik the not-so-great husband stood at the doorway, saying nothing.

"Wow. That was some fracture you had. Your hip joint has completely fallen apart. I think you had a femoral-neck fracture. In defense of your physician at home, sometimes you can't see that break on initial X-rays. Most patients would keep on hurting, and complaining, and return for another visit, when the fracture would probably then be apparent. You didn't see the doctor again, Sara?"

"No. My husband and father told me I had to be tough, that I was a member of the royal family, and that our people had lived and worked in the frozen mountains for hundreds of years with no medical care and did just fine."

With that said, she glanced at her husband. If looks could kill, ol' Erik's family would be making funeral arrangements for him back home.

"Well, sorry to be the bearer of bad news, but your hip needs replacing. If you want to quit hurting, that is."

"Yes, anything. I can't stand it anymore. We're here, Doctor, to get the problem fixed. I don't want to leave for my country and then return. Can you take care of it for me while I'm here?"

"I'd be pleased to do so. Rae my nurse and Fran my . . . assistant . . . will help you and Nabila with the scheduling. It's been a pleasure."

Sara extended her hand, and I shook it gently. Erik turned and walked away in silence.

Nabila, Rae, and I left the exam room to allow Sara some privacy in getting dressed. Nabila then turned to me. "Doctor, I know this will be an imposition, but I would appreciate having your cell phone number. My clients are like my family, and it will be necessary to get directly in touch with you if a problem arises."

I hesitated, then acquiesced. I swear I heard Rae snicker.

CHAPTER 10

TONY'S

Thursday, September 5, 2002

"I'm so glad to be home!" I said to Mary Louise as I entered our apartment. "How's Mother this fine evening?"

"Gone . . . like the wind."

"What? She just got here yesterday. What about the funeral?"

"That's why she left, my sweet. She called Lela Belle and asked her about services for her brother. Lela told her that Rico, the liver donor, would not be able to leave the hospital for a few more days, and that they wanted Howard buried in Zavalla. So, your mother hung up the phone, packed up her things, told me goodbye, said she would see me at the funeral, and left. Tip barked as she exited. I think it was a joyful noise. Your mother hates dogs."

I patted Tip's head, scratched his face with both hands, and wondered how anyone couldn't love this creature.

"And her parting words were something to do with convincing Lela Belle to bring a lawsuit against the hospital for killing her brother."

"What? What is she thinking? Man, those Peck genes. I don't have any of those, do I? Mom is so stubborn, and impetuous, and she won't listen to reason. She just goes off and does what she wants, regardless of the consequences and without regard to interpersonal relationships. And most of her sisters are just like her, downright mean, like a copperhead snake."

"Jim Bob, why don't you go get cleaned up and take me out to dinner? Tomorrow is Friday, your day off, unless some emergency comes in, right? You can make rounds, get your desk cleaned off, and then spend some quality time with your bride in Galveston."

"That sounds great, Mary Louise, but I agreed to meet that lawyer O'Leary at 10 a.m. We probably can't leave before 11. By the way, you didn't answer my question."

"And what question was that, dear?"

"You know, about the genes? The Peck genes?"

She hemmed and hawed for a moment, very unlike her, then quietly said, "I love you with all my heart. You're a fine surgeon and a good human being. We all have genes that we'd prefer not to have. You're no exception."

"Just don't tell me I'm like my mother and her sisters. I couldn't take that, coming from you."

She patted my check and gave me a kiss. I guess that was my answer. How sad to think I was a male version of my outrageous mother and aunts.

On the way to Tony's, we called our son J. J. from the car to see if he might be able to grace us with his presence for dinner. He was always busy, between work and, well, work. He dated but there was no one special in his life, as far as his mother and I knew. And she would know, as those two are very close. Mary Louise knows what's going on with J. J. much more than I do. Amazingly enough, he was free for a couple of hours for dinner. He had to meet some people at a concert and was very excited about the bands that were playing. We hadn't heard of any of them, which was typical. Hoobastank? Saliva?

Seether? What kinds of names were those? What about Waylon Jennings, Willie Nelson, and George Strait? And Charles Brown? And Bobby "Blue" Bland? And Lou Rawls? Those artists' songs would last forever. The kids these days had terrible taste in music, listening to these fly-by-night bands. What a waste. They would all be flashes in the pan, in my opinion. Weezer? Good lord.

Whoa. I sounded like my mother.

J. J. met us at the bar. Jerry, my favorite spirit mixer, entertained us, regaling us with stories of various celebrities—no names, of course—and their antics at Tony's. Mary Louise had her now-usual cosmopolitan (she tried one about a year ago and never looked back), I had a dirty martini up, and J. J. ordered a craft beer. Something new, he said, and the coming thing: microbreweries. Sounded like another flash in the pan to me, but then I once had a chance to invest in the Fidelity Magellan Fund and declined because it didn't sound "traditional." Illustrative of the typical doctor's investment strategy of buy high, sell low.

Tony's is unique. You are supposed to "table hop." That means that, on the way to your assigned table in the main dining area, you must stop and say hello to friends and acquaintances. There is no privacy at Tony's. See and be seen, and visit, that's the tradition. You want privacy? Go to the Blue Lagoon. It's so dark in there you can't see to walk. That's the perfect place to not see and not be seen.

Ruben, our favorite server, greeted us at the table and gave Mary Louise a hug. "So glad to see you back, Mrs. Brady. Many a prayer was said for you after that horrible accident. I see you are without a cane tonight and looking lovely as always."

"Thanks Ruben. I appreciate all those prayers that were said on my behalf. And I'm very glad to be here with my husband and son, and you, my friend. Things could have turned out much differently for me, in so many ways."

He patted her on the shoulder. "Okay, enough maudlin conversation for the evening. This is Tony's! Another drink, or do we want to hear the specials?"

Ruben went through his spiel, and we ordered. We would share the Caesar salad between the three of us. I ordered the veal chop with mushroom risotto. Mary Louise wanted a lobster tail with drawn butter. J. J. wanted that most elaborate of dishes, spaghetti with meatballs, which is one of the best items Tony made. I ordered a bottle of Chianti Classico Ruffino Ducale Gold, my personal favorite, to be served with dinner.

Once we had our food, Tony came out of the kitchen, greeted us, and hugged Mary Louise. "So glad to see you back in action, my darling. You were missed, and many prayers were said for your speedy recovery. You are looking spectacularly gorgeous this evening."

That she was, by the way. She had her blond hair up with some sort of rhinestone hairband, which seemed to hold all that thick beautiful hair in place. She had on a beautiful red Chanel suit, her nails done in a matching color. She was a knockout, and I doubt anyone would think she was over fifty years old.

"So, J. J., I'd like to ask you a favor."

He looked at his mother and shook his head. "This sounds expensive."

She smiled, and said, "Just listen to your dad."

I told him the story that my Uncle Howard had related to me the day before his liver transplant and, unfortunately, his demise.

"Dad, I'm sorry, but why would you want to honor a request from Uncle Howard after his death? According to what you just told me, he hadn't told Aunt Lela Belle, nor his two sons. You're the only person who knows about this alleged murder of his friend. Why not just let it die with him? What possible good could come from dredging up some terrible event from the past?"

"Well, son, I feel an obligation to him. He chose me and only me to tell this secret to. And his parting words implied that if in fact he didn't survive the liver transplant, he wanted to make amends. And I believe he wanted me to make amends for him if he didn't make it. I feel I'm honor-bound to discover what happened. What I'll do with any information I discover, well, I'll have to decide that, if and when any discoveries are made. Which is where you come in."

"So, Pops, you're hoping that I'll employ the use of Brad's and my company to do a lot of the legwork for you?"

"Well, you've helped me immensely in the past, and God knows you pulled out the stops to find out who was behind your mother's hit-and-run accident last year."

"That was about Mom, and that's not fair. I would do anything for her. I don't even know your Uncle Howard."

"OUR Uncle Howard, my uncle and your great-uncle. He was family. Not your mom, but still family."

"Dad, this is a touchy subject, but it's well known that you don't even like your mother, and Howard was her brother. And I've heard some stories that you used to tell about how he was a drunk and would show up at your house when you were a kid, and—"

"And yes, that's all true."

"And you still want me to commit resources to another one of your wild projects?"

"Yes."

"This is going to cost you."

"What??? You've never charged me before!"

"Dad, the past is the past. B&B Investigations is a thriving concern, with all sorts of contracts involving corporate espionage, political intrigue, and governmental skulduggery. We have over twenty employees, a huge payroll, and ridiculous lease-space costs. Brad and I have made an agreement: no more freebies, especially for family. Sorry."

"How about a dad's discount?"

Dinner ended on an amicable note, despite the bickering between J. J. and me. Mary Louise finally resolved the situation, as usual. I would be responsible for obtaining baseline information about the past exploits of Uncle Howard, and B&B would check out and evaluate data as it was presented to them on a somewhat discounted basis.

"I'll be paying for all this in retirement savings," I whined, as Mary Louise and I slipped under the covers, finally at home and in bed. Tip had done his business quickly, anxious for quality time with Mom and Dad.

"You can afford it, husband of mine. Don't forget I worked for a living for a long time, and I can make you a loan from time to time as need be."

"Great. And what do I pay you back with?"

"Oh, I'll think of something," she said, as she turned out the light.

CHAPTER 11

DR. JEFF CLARKE

Friday, September 6, 2002

With no surgical emergencies to add on to my standard Friday-light schedule, the house staff and I met for rounds late for us, at 7 a.m. Nurse Gwen was busy with the daily information exchange during shift change, so we were on our own. Both Tim and Shelley had been on call the night before. There had been so many emergencies and admissions that both had slept in the call-room area, spartan rooms consisting of bunk beds and a bathroom in each. Both looked like zombies. I recognized that look all too well, having endured six years of postgraduate surgical training myself.

There had been no catastrophes during the night involving my patients. Everyone was recovering well, taking their meds, participating in physical therapy as instructed, and generally getting better. The folks who had to stay in the hospital over the weekend got a little clingy during Friday morning rounds. Knowing that I would be off Saturday and Sunday, they would make little comments like these:

"Hope you have a nice weekend. I'll be here eating this slop called hospital food."

"Must be nice to have two or three days off. I'll be tortured by the physical therapist while you'll be out, what, sailing your yacht I paid for?"

"What kind of children-you-call-doctors will be looking out for me while you're out galivanting around town having fun?"

And on it went. Normal Friday morning banter between patient and surgeon.

As we were walking back to the nursing station, my beeper went off. It was my office.

"Morning, Fran. How's everything over there?"

"Peachy so far. Done with rounds yet?"

"Just now. Thought I would get a bite to eat before I come over to the office and, I promise, clear my desk."

"I'll hold you to that. I just got a call from the pathology department. They're starting the autopsy on your Uncle Howard at 8:30. Figured you'd want to save yourself a mile or two of walking and stay over at the hospital for the procedure before heading this way. Not that you couldn't lose a few pounds, Pop."

"Funny. Real funny. Okay, I'll do as you say . . . skinny."

"See you in a while, Porky. And don't forget the lawyer meeting at ten."

Fran always managed to get the last word in.

After breakfast in the surgical lounge, I wandered down through the bowels of University Hospital into the basement area where the pathology department was located. I found a living person, who gave me directions to the autopsy area. She said Mr. Peck was assigned to table 24, and that Dr. Clarke was in charge of the case.

"You know of course that Dr. Clarke is now assistant chief of the pathology department and also deputy medical examiner for Harris County?"

"What? But he's always been so . . . outspoken and all. Doesn't the medical examiner have to have some social skills or people skills or something, to allow him to speak to the media in a civilized fashion?"

"Apparently not," she responded.

I finally found my destination and entered a massive room with a two-story ceiling, with all the plumbing pipes and electrical wiring exposed. There had to be thirty or so examining tables, with most surrounded by at least one pathologist and an assistant. The stench was unbearable, from both the preservative formaldehyde and the decaying body parts and internal fluids. I found a box of masks, applied two, and added a gown, surgical cap, and shoe covers—well, in my case, boot covers. I wandered around, looking for table 24 as instructed, when I heard a loud voice:

"Brady, over here."

I worked my way around the tables and found my old medical school friend and confidant Dr. Jeff Clarke. His Coke-bottle glasses were missing, and his wild curly red hair almost looked tame under his paper hat.

"Jeff old buddy, congratulations on your new appointment. I'm happy for you, but somewhat surprised. You never seemed to be, how shall I put it, the administrative type. And look at you, all cleaned up and dignified looking."

"Well, Brady, people change, and I finally decided that if I wanted to make a difference in things around here, I would have to accomplish it from the inside.

"I can't wait to hear your first press conference. I hear you got Mr. Peck's autopsy assignment?"

"That I did, friend. He was your uncle?"

"Small world around here. Word travels fast."

"You bet. Want to see what I found?"

"Sure. How can you stand this smell? What do you have on, just one mask?"

"Been doing this over twenty years. My olfactory receptors died a long time ago, Jim Bob. Can't smell a thing, which is good down here, but bad when you want to enjoy some fettuccine with Alfredo sauce. Without being able to smell, I really can't taste much, either. Sucks being me, huh?"

"Sorry to hear, Jeff. So, what did you find?"

"Get a little closer and take a look. I put the liver transplant back in position so you can appreciate the anatomy. I have the major vessels in and out of the liver marked with tape, and the hepatic ducts as well. So, I'll lift the liver out now and set it aside, so you can see underneath. Bend over a little more and look down in the hole behind where the liver was. Do you see that reddish mass with dried blood around it?"

"Yes. Is that the head of the pancreas?"

"Bingo. Attaboy, you still remember some of the basics. Okay, I'm going to expose the pancreatic head a little better and show you something."

He started mobilizing the pancreas, made a cut or two, then lifted the front portion of the organ out and set it on a stainless-steel side table.

"What do you think, Brady?"

"I have no idea, Jeff. What is it?"

"Look at this section here," he said, as he pointed with an instrument to a different-colored section of the organ. "Not the same color as the rest of the pancreas, is it?"

"No."

"So, I've taken some sections of tissue and looked at them under the microscope. It's cancer of the head of the pancreas, no doubt about it."

"Jeff, wait a minute. I looked through Howard's chart and talked to him the night before surgery. He had cirrhosis of the liver, and also a small cancer in the liver, but he had extensive studies—CT scans, MRI scans, PET scans—all looking for any sort of metastases, which of course would preclude him having the liver transplant in the first place. All the tests were negative."

"The tests were wrong, or they were misinterpreted, in which case this will create a helluva lawsuit. He had a separate primary adenocarcinoma of the pancreas, not a metastasis. This lesion was not seen on any of the tests, according to the chart. I haven't seen the scans myself, which I can assure you I will do before I sign off on the cause of death. But this cancer was hiding in plain sight, so to speak. Basically, while the liver transplant was being done, and Dr. Crawford was in there moving things around, clamping and cutting this and sewing that, he disturbed this lesion in the pancreas, and it started to bleed. You know the pancreas is a very vascular organ, and once the wound started to well up with blood from the cancer lesion, it would have been almost impossible to contain the hemorrhaging. Especially if there was any damage to the superior mesenteric artery, which there was."

"So, you're saying that if the oncologist and surgeon had known about this lesion, the transplant never would have happened?"

"Exactly. Your uncle was a goner, regardless of whether the transplant was successful or not. This was a stage 4 adenocarcinoma of the pancreas. And the procedure was a waste of good tissue from the donor. I understand the donor was a family member?"

"Yes, his son."

"Well, Brady, it's a damn good thing the liver regenerates. Too bad, though, that he went through all that for nothing."

CHAPTER 12

THOMAS O'LEARY

Friday, September 6, 2002

I arrived at my office around nine thirty, anxious to get the lawyer meeting over with and be on the road with Mary Louise and Tip and start relaxing in Galveston. As I walked past the many desks and cubicles throughout the University Orthopedic Clinic, I got some weird looks. Finally, someone clamped their nose, and I realized the problem—odor hangover from the autopsy.

I tried to sneak into my office without drawing attention from Fran and Rae, but they were too quick.

"My God, go take a shower. You're going to stink up the whole clinic," Fran exclaimed.

"I think we have some Raid around here. Better that than the smell currently attached to you," Rae said.

"Okay, okay. I'll go shower. Can you get me some clean scrubs please? Is the lawyer here?"

"Yep, just waiting on you, boss man."

Shower done, hair washed, I did smell a little better, at least good enough to go back to my office, clear my desk, and meet a lawyer who wanted to discuss "personal matters." Of course, to emphasize the extent of my previous stinkiness, both Rae and Fran had binder clips over their respective noses.

"Funny, ladies, so funny. Fran, put the lawyer in the conference room, please."

There was a small conference room set up next to my office, used primarily by me, containing a blond wood table that sat six people, with Western and Native American art scattered along the three walls. On the south side of the room there was a large glass window facing the medical center, with a view of the domed stadium in the distance.

Fran escorted a small man through the entry door. "Morning, Dr. Brady, I'm Thomas O'Leary," he said, as he extended his hand.

He appeared to be in his sixties, mostly bald, with a somewhat wrinkled suit and a white shirt, sans tie. The suit was definitely not designer. He was five foot nine inches or so and had large horn-rimmed glasses and a smiling face. He seemed harmless, but you couldn't be too careful, him being an attorney and all. But he did wear Western boots, so that was in his favor.

Fran asked, "Something to drink, sir?"

"I'd love a coffee black, if it's not too much trouble."

"Coming right up. Doc?"

"Just a bottled water, thanks."

She left the conference room and returned shortly with the requested beverages and shut the door.

"Well it is certainly nice to meet you, Doctor. Your reputation precedes you—in a good way, of course."

"That's very kind of you, Mr. O'Leary. So, what can I do for you, sir?"

"Just call me Tom, please. Less formal, and as you can see from my attire, I'm not one of the corporate types from one of the white-shoe firms. I have a unique practice and have the pleasure and luxury to represent a small group of families in all their business endeavors and with their estate planning."

He opened a worn briefcase and pulled out a stack of papers. "This is a somewhat awkward situation and, of course, complicated, as awkward situations often are. Do you remember Harold Sanders, a patient of yours?"

I thought for a moment. "You mean the fellow that was shot in the leg on a hunting trip, who later died of an overwhelming infection? Who was on the University Hospital board?"

"Yes, sir, he's the one."

"That had to be ten years ago."

"Yes, 1992."

"What could I possibly have to do with Mr. Sanders at this late date? The statute of limitation has run out on malpractice, hasn't it?"

He laughed. "Yes, but this has nothing to do with malpractice. Mr. and Mrs. Sanders admired you tremendously and were grateful for the care you provided to Mr. Sanders. Prior to his death, in fact, he added a codicil to his will, naming you as a beneficiary. It was signed by him and his wife."

"A beneficiary? You've got to be kidding. Besides, that was ten years ago. I would think his estate has been settled for years."

"You are correct, sir. The estate has been settled for years, except for your, shall we say, inheritance."

"I can't imagine Mr. Sanders remembering me in his will. Is Mrs. Sanders still alive?"

"Oh, yes. She's carried the torch for you all these years and was totally opposed by their three children over what they think was a last-minute decision made by a man deranged by a systemic infection and multiple medications."

"You mean the children were opposed to the bequest?"

"Oh yes, but Mrs. Sanders was determined to see you received what her husband felt was an important gift. You see, the children filed a lawsuit against the estate to prevent you from receiving this gift. What they didn't know what that their father, that sly old bastard—and I use that term with the highest affection—had signed another codicil to his will, which stated that anyone who challenged his will would be disinherited until such time as the individual agreed to the terms of the will."

"Are you telling me it's taken this long to resolve the terms of the will?"

"The wheels of justice turn slowly, Dr. Brady. At any rate, now that we've met and know each other, I want you to review all this paperwork. You're going to have many questions, and you might want to seek legal counsel regarding the terms of your inheritance. Once you've done that and understand the legalese, I'd like to meet again."

With that, he stood, shook my hand, and headed for the door.

"Can't you even tell me what the gift entails, Tom?"

He paused, looked at me, and said, "Land, sir. Valuable land."

I whipped through signing charts in about a half hour and dictated a few reports to insurance-company physician-executives who had denied approval of upcoming surgeries. This was a common occurrence, unfortunately. These delay tactics cost the patient time and money, while I guess the insurance companies were making double compound interest on the billions they had sequestered away in investment portfolios. The way I saw the future of medical and surgical care, the problem was only going to worsen.

As I walked out of the office to tell my staff goodbye, my cell phone rang.

Thinking that it was Mary Louise wanting to know when I'd be home, I answered "Hello, sweet thing."

"Uh, Dr. Brady? This is Nabila. I brought Sara in to see you yesterday?"

"Yes, sorry, I thought it was my wife calling. We're headed to Galveston today."

"Sorry to disturb you, Doctor, but Sara has developed rather severe abdominal pain. It looks to me like appendicitis but could be a ruptured ovarian cyst or some sort of bowel obstruction. I need you to recommend a surgeon."

"Are you a nurse, Nabila?"

"Yes, sir."

"I didn't realize that. You introduced yourself as the translator, so I had no idea. That's great to know. Listen, the guy I want to see Sara is Dewey Moss. Do you know him?"

"Only by reputation, sir."

"Well, he's a little bit of a cowboy, but there is no better surgeon anywhere. Let me try and get hold of him. Where are you and Sara?"

"In the emergency room."

"I'll get right back to you. Give me your number, please."

I wrote it down, and before I could tell Fran to get hold of Dewey, she was already talking to his office staff. I loved it. Efficiency at its finest.

"He's in surgery, Pops, but will be out in a half hour. His people will get him to the ER as soon as he's done."

"Thanks much. I need to get going. I think ol' Dew can handle Nabila and Sara. Don't know about Erik, though. He's probably never seen anyone like Dewey Moss."

Neither had I, until 1972.

CHAPTER 13

JULY 1, 1972

Saturday, July 1, 1972

I graduated medical school on June 30, 1972. Medical school is like college for the first two years. You have your cadaver, which you share with three other med students and dissect on all year. You learn most everything about anatomy of the human body from your cadaver, which becomes your best friend. Then you have those medically related sciences you have to learn about—physiology, microbiology, biochemistry, pharmacology. This takes up about 90 percent of the first two years of medical school. The last two years of medical school are basically clinical, meaning you work under interns, residents, fellows, and attending staff in the process of learning how to diagnose and treat patients.

Med students are on the bottom rung of the ladder. The patient contact you have is as an underling in most every situation. You make rounds in the hospital with the house staff and attending staff, and you try to glean information about medical diseases while being grilled by all those on the ladder above you regarding said diseases which you don't know anything about, which is why you're on rounds in the first place.

The kinds of activities that the med student is allowed to do include doing histories and physicals on clinic patients and hospital in-patients, drawing blood, and starting IVs the nurses couldn't start, which are always impossible, otherwise the nurse would have been able to do it. And, when assigned to the ER at the University General Hospital, you spend your time in the suture room, once it has been determined by the upper-level staff that there is no damage to the patient's anatomy other than the skin laceration. Most of these patients have lacerations because they were either drunk or high and, as a result, engaged in all sorts of nefarious activities. Many are hand-cuffed to the bed, police officers at the ready, so one can imagine the pleasantries of conversation while a greenhorn med student is trying to inject a local anesthetic into a wound so it can be sutured while the patient is screaming and cursing at said med student. I always felt safer sewing up the ones in handcuffs.

Most of us in my med school class tried to quit at least one hundred times, but the Selective Service System (the Draft) kept us rooted in place. Rooted yes, happy no.

And so it was, in the very early morning hours of July 1, 1972, that I entered the emergency room of the University General Hospital, also fondly known as the Houston Knife and Gun Club. That would be my first rotation out of med school—yesterday I was just a med student, and eighteen hours later I was a real doctor for the first time, a brand-new resident, and I didn't have a clue as to what I was doing. The good news was that I had a third-year resident scheduled to be in charge, someone I could learn from, who would kindly cover up any mistakes I might make, be a bud, and nurse me along while I got my feet wet for the next two months, the length of the ER rotation.

I searched the ER for the upper-level resident—his name was Nathan, but I didn't know if that was his first or last—who was in charge, but he was nowhere to be found. I asked one of the nursing staff about the man, and she said with a snicker, "check the call room." So, I merrily located and entered the call room, saw Dr. Nathan, and introduced myself. He looked up at me and said:

"Brady, ever heard of the Berry Plan?"

"Yes. It's a military deferment plan, right? It allows you to complete med school, internship, and residency prior to beginning your service obligation."

"Very good, and as a third-year surgical resident, my services are also in high demand in Southeast Asia, right? But, hey, I'm in the Berry Plan, so I don't have to worry, which is why I signed up. I have to give Uncle Sam four years of military service, but I'll be able to do that as a fully trained surgeon, because I'm in the Berry Plan."

The Berry Plan was a Vietnam War-era program that allowed physicians to defer their obligatory military service until they had completed medical school and residency training. I hadn't signed up for it because I got drafted right before I graduated medical school. However, once the army doc did my physical and discovered I'd had rheumatic fever at the age of twelve, he classified me 4-F. It didn't matter I had no symptoms or residual effects, not even a heart murmur from the strep-throat-related disease; I was out, and end of discussion. A lot of my colleagues had signed up for the Berry Plan, however, and it was the best deal going, in most circumstances.

Nathan handed me a letter. I read it over and began to feel turbulence developing in the depth of my bowels. "This letter says you are to report immediately to Fort Hood to prepare for deployment . . . to Viet Nam."

"That's right, rookie. I'm out of here, going to Nam. There's a 20 percent chance I won't survive, did you know that?"

"No." I thought about joking that those were better odds than I'd be facing, trying to survive this two-month rotation without a senior resident running the show, but his actual threatened existence made me swallow my words. "How am I supposed to do this job without a senior resident in charge?"

He looked at me, laughed, and said, "Everybody has a cross to bear, as the Allman Brothers sang, man. Good luck."

And he was gone.

I was still in a state of disbelief when one of the nursing staff knocked on the call-room door, opened it, and said, "Doc Brady?"

"That's me."

"Well, they tell me you're now in charge of the ER, so let's make rounds on the patients out here and get a report from the night shift."

And so my two months as the impromptu head of the University General Hospital Emergency Room began. The nursing staff was very helpful, orienting me to all the equipment and special rooms, radiology, the lab, and the various and sundry dos and don'ts and the politics thereof. Most importantly, since the house-staff shifts were twenty-four-hours long, the absolute MUST was to rest when you could.

As I was headed to the call room for a nap, one of the nurses stopped me.

"GSW on the way, Rook. Get your butt to the shock room."

"GSW?"

She stared at me for a moment and said, "Oh dear God."

I followed her to the shock room. There was no patient yet, but there were half a dozen staff standing in wait, holding IV tubes, endotracheal tubes, cardiac monitoring devices, pulse oximeters—all the devices necessary to keep the patient alive from the GSW, which I discovered meant gunshot wound. The team consisted of an anesthesiologist, two internists, a perfusionist, and two nurses. Word from the fire department was that the patient was being airlifted in via helicopter, had a chest wound of some sort, and had lost a lot of blood.

We all looked upward subconsciously as we collectively heard the rumble of the chopper. The pilot had to carefully land on the heliport, located on the top floor, which was the tenth floor, and in the middle of a group of buildings that were all too close to the heliport. The EMTs then had to transport the patient via a dedicated elevator down to the shock room on the first floor, adjacent to the ambulance entrance.

When the patient arrived, everyone went into action except me. I had no idea what my role was at that point. The staff all knew by then it was my first day, and that Rook, short for Rookie, was my new name. I basically stood in place, watching the action, waiting for instructions. The patient's clothes were cut off with scissors. There were three other docs in the room who knew what to do and went about their work. Intravenous and arterial lines were started, a urinary catheter was inserted, and the patient was intubated and hooked up to Oxygen.

"Pressure's down to 60/40. Pulse rising."

"Hang some blood. He's bleeding like hell."

"Rook, you're gonna have to look at that wound. This would be a good time," someone said.

I moved to the patient's left side, lifted the bulky bandages over the chest, and noted several small towels underneath caked with blood. It looked for a moment like the blood vessels had clotted, but then I saw bright-red blood start pumping from a small wound in the upper part of the chest, just below the clavicle, or collar bone.

"I see the wound, but it's pumping like hell. How do I get to it?"

Someone said, "You have to open the chest. Ever done that?"

"Gross anatomy class two years ago. Is there a real surgeon around anywhere, like upstairs in the OR? I need some help here, people."

One of the staff called to the operating room, then said, "Dr. Moss is up there operating on a ruptured aneurysm. He said to put you on speaker."

"Hello?"

"Hey, Rook, got a little action goin' down there?"

"Yes, sir, I have a patient with a GSW to the upper left chest, oozing bright-red blood. Pressure is down, we're pumping in blood, but I don't think he's going to make it unless we stop the bleeding."

"That's right, Rook, you gotta open his chest. Get a scalpel and an 11 blade. Make an incision starting at the entry wound and curve it around his nipple and into the armpit. Clamp the bleeders, put in a rib retractor, and tell me what you see."

I glanced at the nurse beside me while she grabbed a sterile tray full of instruments, opened it, and waited. I grabbed the scalpel, attached the blade, and made the cut as Dr. Moss had described. This produced even more bleeding, so I clamped multiple bleeders, shoved in the rib spreader, and turned the crank. Somebody hooked up some plastic tubing and started sucking blood out of the depths of the wound.

"Are you still on speaker?" I asked.

"Yep. What do you see? I'm betting a hole in the pulmonary artery."

"Yes. I see the artery. It has a small hole in the top portion, like a crease. Really is pumping blood. Also, the lung is collapsed. Looks like a deflated tire."

"Forget the lung. Once the blood is out of the chest cavity, it will start to expand. Clamp the artery, one on each side of the hole."

I did that. Suddenly there was no bleeding. I saw the lung begin to expand. I looked at the cardiac monitors, and the patient's pressure was creeping upward.

"Done. Lung's expanding, pressure's rising. Now what?"

"Get your ass up here to the OR. You walk beside the stretcher, and don't let those clamps move!"

And that's what we did, and slowly. We caught the elevator and rose to the second floor. As soon as the door opened, we were surrounded by staff. I kept my hands as still as possible as the stretcher rolled into the OR. The staff transferred the patient to the operating table, which was a tricky maneuver, considering I was on the patient's left side and holding onto those two pulmonary artery clamps for dear life.

Once the patient was on the table, the OR door burst open and Dr. Dewey Moss strode in. The only more welcome sight to me at that moment would have been Jesus. Dr. Moss slipped around me and looked into the wound.

"Good job, Rook. Now I'm going to place my hands on the clamps, and once I have them, back away."

I did that and stepped out of his way, and he went to work. I was shaking like a leaf at that point and emotionally overwrought. I watched him for a few minutes, then felt a nudge from one of the nurses that had assisted in transporting the patient upstairs.

"Great job, Rook, but we have to get back downstairs. You have an ER to run."

CHAPTER 14

PLAINVIEW

Friday, September 6, 2002

That incident began a twenty-five-year friendship with Dr. Dewey Moss. I had referred him countless patients over the years, and he had returned the favor. We were social friends on occasion as well, but he and I had a bond that was unbreakable. He had saved my butt in my hour of need, and I would never forget it.

I went home, changed, and packed the car, and Mary Louise, Tip, and I headed for Galveston. Before I could broach the subject of my meeting with lawyer O'Leary, Dewey called me.

"Well, Jim Bob, I LOVE this Princess Sara. We're going to get along just fine. Can't say much for the husband, though. She's got a hot appendix, about to rupture I think, so we're headed to the OR. Sorry to put that hip replacement off, but this is an emergency."

"No problem at all. Do what you have to do. And Dew, thanks again for bailing me out in 1972."

"Brady, that was a lifetime ago. You've said that to me probably a hundred times."

"Yeah, but I was just reminiscing about the old days, and 'good ol' Dewey from St. Louie.'"

He laughed. "You on the way to G-town?"

"Yep."

"Got M. L. in the car?"

"Yep."

"Put her on speaker phone."

"Hello, Dewey."

"Hello, beautiful. Just wanted to remind you that if anything happens to that husband of yours, I want to be first in line."

"Dewey, you have a beautiful wife and family."

"Just sayin', M. L. I think your man is cracking up. Give him a good weekend and send him back in better shape. He's mumbling about things from thirty years ago."

"I'll do my best. Bye now, Dewey."

As we were driving, Mary Louise asked where I was going.

"Galveston. Why?"

"Well, normally we take either the 610 Loop or Highway 59 and intersect with Interstate 45 and take the direct route. You're headed to Highway 288, which goes down to Freeport and Lake Jackson, what is locally known as the back way. I realize you can then go through the San Luis Pass and get to Jamaica Beach from the west end; it just takes a little longer."

"Well, I was worried about traffic, seeing as how it's almost noon on a Friday. Thought it might be fun to go this way, maybe stop at Surfside and eat at Kitty's Purple Cow."

"Hmm. Wasn't that where your Uncle Howard told you he had shot his best friend?"

"You're right. I had forgotten about that."

"Jim Bob Brady, you didn't forget. You're trying to get some information on that shooting, not that anyone working there could possibly remember an event that happened, what, thirty years ago? A long time ago."

"Well, the thought did cross my mind, sweetie."

She gave me a long, baleful look, then sighed. "You're too much. By the way, what did that lawyer want?"

"You won't believe it. I have a sheaf of papers to go through, and hopefully you'll help me. I'm not of a legal mind, so to speak. Bottom line is that Harold Sanders, my former patient who passed away after that hunting accident, named me in his will."

"Jim Bob, that was what, seven or eight years ago?"

"There's a story behind it. The papers are in my briefcase in the back seat. Feel free to start reading. We can discuss it when we get home."

Kitty's was aptly named. The building was purple. It was about one thirty on Friday, and most of the outdoor tables were full. Kitty's was in Surfside, not on the beach, but close enough to have a distant view of the confluence of Galveston Bay and the Gulf of Mexico. We wandered inside, ordered our burgers, got a couple of beers, and took a number. We went back outdoors to find a table, and by chance one was being cleared. We deeply breathed in the humid, briny air, sighed, and tapped our ice-cold bottles.

The food came out shortly, and it was delicious. We had ordered double-meat double cheeseburgers with fries and onion rings. It probably wasn't good for him, but I ordered a double-meat burger for Tip, sans lettuce, tomato, pickles, cheese, bun, and sauce. Good thing we only had a half-hour drive to the beach house. The deck was calling me for a nap in the hammock. Tip was already dozing, having swallowed his lunch almost whole.

When the young lady brought our check, I asked her how long she had worked at Kitty's.

"Since I was fourteen. My granny was the original owner, and I've been working here off and on as long as I can remember. I'm married and have kids now, so I only fill in when the place is short of help."

"Reason I ask is that my uncle used to come here a long time ago and told me of a shooting that happened."

"A shooting? I don't know anything about that, but it was probably long before my time. I'm sure my Gran would know about that, though."

"Is she here, by any chance?"

"Oh lord, no. She's in a nursing home over in Lake Jackson. Has a memory problem, if you know what I mean."

"I'm sorry to hear that. What's the name of the facility, if you don't mind me asking?"

"Plainview, although it has no view, as far as I can tell. Why do you ask, sir?"

"Well, I'd really like to get some information about this shooting. Truth is, it's a family matter, and I'm trying to gain some closure for my uncle's children," I lied. "I was hoping that someone here might be able to help me out."

"Did your uncle shoot someone here?"

"Possibly, but the details are somewhat sketchy. The two fellows involved were what used to be called hobos, men of the road and rail."

"Oh, you mean like those old winos that used to hang out here."

"Well, that would be correct. What do you know about those folk?"

"Oh, it's just that when I was a kid, we had some of those men as customers. I was scared to death of them, but Gran thought they were harmless. They just came here to get a good meal. She called them 'her boys.' She used to tell me she must have the best food around because her boys would hitchhike all the way from Galveston to eat here."

Plainview Retirement Home was only ten miles from Kitty's, so we made the trip after lunch. It was a squat, flat-roofed building, painted beige but weather-worn from the various hurricanes and storms that have plagued the Gulf Coast since time began. Inside was painted a drab beige as well, and upon entry into the building, we strolled into what was probably called a "great room." Mary Louise and I noted twenty or thirty older folks slumped over in wheelchairs, some drooling, with the television tuned to an obnoxiously loud game show. It was, to say the least, depressing.

I approached a young woman at a semicircular desk not unlike those found at nurses' stations at the hospital.

"Morning. We're here to see Evelyn Jacoby."

"Family or friends?"

"Friends," I exaggerated.

"Visiting hours are almost over. You'll have to be quick. Take a walk through our great room, then down the hall to Room 112."

Nursing homes have an odor about them. I don't know exactly what from, but I presume it has something to do with a combination of dysfunctional bowels and bladders in the aged patient population. More depressing thoughts.

We reached 112, knocked, and entered to find a semiprivate room decorated with what I assumed were family pictures on both sides of the curtain dividing the two halves of the space. The woman we wanted to speak with was in the far bed by the window. We noted the roommate was sleeping and snoring loudly.

Evelyn Jacoby was awake and staring out the sole window. She looked to be in her eighties, with white hair and a sad look on her wrinkled face.

"Mrs. Jacoby?"

"Yes?"

"Hello. I'm Dr. Jim Brady, and this is my wife, Mary Louise."

"Hello, dear," she said, directing her greeting to Mary Louise and extending her hand. I didn't hold much interest for her. "You look so much like my daughter. But you're not, are you?"

"No ma'am, I'm not. How are you feeling today?"

"Not too bad, dear. Just waiting here to die and see my friends that have gone on before me."

"Well, we won't keep you long, but your granddaughter at Kitty's thought you might be able to help us out with something."

"She's so lovely, comes to see me often. And what's that, dear, that I might be able to help you with?"

"Many years ago, my husband's uncle was involved in a shooting at Kitty's, and your granddaughter thought you might remember what happened."

Mrs. Jacoby was pensive and silent, and she stared at Mary Louise. "Mutt and Jeff," she said.

"I'm sorry?"

"Mutt and Jeff. They used to come every so often, hitchhiked from Galveston. They were railroad boys. Used to ride those rails all over the place. They'd end up in Galveston, get a hankerin' for my cookin' and would just show up, come all that way for a meal."

"Why do you call them Mutt and Jeff?"

"One was tall, one was short. The tall one was homely and rough around the edges. The short one was a looker, seemed to have a way with the ladies, and was very polite. Like he had a good upbringing but was down on his luck. I didn't know their real names."

"Evelyn, you have a pretty good memory for someone who is in this retirement home in the memory-care area."

"Dear, I can remember things that happened fifty years ago, but I'm sorry to say I can't remember to go to the toilet when I should."

Mary Louise patted her arm. "Do you remember anything about the shooting?"

"Well, the boys had just gotten their food. All of a sudden, I heard loud arguing and saw Mutt, the tall one, with a gun in his hand. Then Jeff, the short one, tried to grab it away. They wrestled, and the gun went off. Next thing I know, Mutt is on the ground and Jeff is high-tailin' it out of there. I called the operator for the fire department. The Surfside firemen were there in a jiffy—the station is just down the road—and they worked on him, got him in the ambulance and drove away."

CHAPTER 15

GALVESTON COUNTRY CLUB

Friday, September 6, 2002

I so wanted to make a side trip to the Surfside beach fire station, but fatigue, compounded by having eaten every morsel of the double cheeseburger and fries . . . and most of the onion rings . . . and a beer . . . overcame that desire. We drove straight to the weekend house we owned on Indian Beach, unloaded the car posthaste, and scurried to our respective nap sites. Mary Louise took the king bed in the master overlooking the Gulf of Mexico. I opted for the hammock on the upper deck, shaded by the roofline and a large palm tree. Tip opted for the cool spot underneath the hammock. The ocean breeze and surf sounds put me out in nothing flat.

We both awoke at dusk, feeling woozy and, yes, hungry. How was that possible? The sun was fading into the west, and although the beach house faced southeast, we could see the ambient light changing quickly. In California, we would be looking for the green flash as the sun settled into the Pacific Ocean.

"What's for dinner?" I asked jokingly of Mary Louise.

I got the "look."

"I'm up for another chef's cooking. How about you?" she said.

"Perfect. I'll see if we can get into the Galveston Country Club for dinner so we can get some of those incredible soft-shell crabs."

I called, booked a table, and headed for the shower. Clean and refreshed, I poured myself a glass of Rombauer chardonnay, and one for Mary Louise as well. She was sequestered in her bath—the door was still closed—but that didn't stop me from trying to get a peep at her in an unknown state of dress. I knocked but then quickly opened the slider, hoping to get a glimpse of my bride of thirty-one years.

"I have wine for you."

"Thanks, and I think I might have missed your knock," she said, as I handed her the crystal stem glass.

She was not undressed, nor was she dressed. In other words, perfect timing on my part. We clinked glasses. I ogled.

"See anything you like?"

"You bet."

"Maybe if you don't run off and start investigating some elusive mystery, you might get to see even more."

"Nash Bridges is off duty for the evening, my dear."

"Bye now," she said, as she shooed me out of the bathroom and shut the door. Darn the luck.

I turned on some Charles Brown blues, made my way to an outdoor Adirondack chair, and drank my wine and listened to the waves butt against the shore. The wine was so good, I had to pour myself a second glass. I had to be mindful of my alcohol intake, however. The Galveston Police Department. Didn't take kindly to its citizens driving around over the limit. Being friends with Stan Lombardo, Chief of the Houston Police Department, wouldn't do me much good down here. I carried in my wallet a typed business card signed by him, addressed to law enforcement in general, that asked that Dr. Jim Bob Brady be shown every courtesy possible. In these parts, that document would probably be used for toilet paper.

Mary Louise exited the bedroom wearing a stunning lavender sundress with matching heels. Her hair was up, and I wondered how in the world she tamed all that unruly blond hair to stay on top of her head. That was one of the little mysteries of life regarding women that men are not now, nor will they ever be, privy to.

Galveston Country Club sat on Stewart Road, about ten minutes from our house. It's the oldest country club in Texas, built in a Mediterranean style and set among palm trees and beautifully man-icured gardens. The golf is challenging, with quite a few water holes, as one would expect from an ocean course. The wind always seemed to be a factor, since Mother Nature had deemed it would always be blowing into the golfer's face.

The hostess greeted Mary Louise and I and showed us to our table. We opted for alfresco dining in a small area that was sheltered by overhead beams covered with roses. Nearby, a piano player plied his trade on a small digital piano with a pair of speakers that pro-duced a clear and resonant sound. It was a perfect table, on a perfect night, with the perfect woman.

Our waitress arrived and offered us water or something stronger. I opted for stronger, and ordered a bottle of Grgich Hills Chardonnay, assuming we both would be eating seafood. She returned, opened the wine, and offered me a taste. I deferred to Mary Louise, the chardon-nay expert.

"Wonderful," she responded. She clinked my glass, and we sipped. I suggested we order, thoughts of seeing my wife in all her undressed splendor foremost in my mind. I ordered the soft-shell crab, she the lobster, and a crab Louie salad to share.

"You love it down here, don't you M. L.?"

"I do. We've been coming to this city for quite a few years. Now that we're playing golf, though, it seems we don't just sit and enjoy the view much anymore."

"True that. Golf takes four or five hours to play and is pretty exhausting."

A few years ago, we accompanied friends on a trip to Telluride, Colorado. We stayed at a resort called the Peaks, and what an experience that was. My friend told me upon arrival that he had booked a tee time for the four of us the next day. I responded that Mary Louise and I didn't play golf. He in turn told me that we did now. And we were both hooked after that weekend. Mary Louise was now a little tentative because of all her injuries from the auto crash last year, but she was a natural at golf. In her younger days she played tennis, and it was apparently an easy progression. As for me, I played baseball as a kid, so I gripped the golf clubs with a two-handed grip and swung out of my shoes on every shot, in case I made contact. I could hit the ball, but it wasn't pretty.

"Some friends at work told me about a place about an hour west of Austin called Horseshoe Bay Resort," I said. "There are three or four golf courses and several good restaurants. Also, the place sits adjacent to Lake LBJ, a constant-level lake about twenty miles long, and has condos right on the water."

"We should try it sometime. Although you won't like that drive, either leaving on Friday or returning home on Sunday. It would probably take at least four hours each way, don't you think? That's one of the reasons why we bought in Galveston, remember?"

"Yep, you're right about that. Still . . . maybe we could explore Horseshoe Bay when I have an extra day or two off, huh?"

"Where you go, I go, husband. I love you," and she clinked my glass again.

"Did you get much reading done in the car? I was distracted."

"Some, and I must say, it was exciting."

"Really? He left me some land, according to O'Leary."

"That's true. But what's important is what that land sits on."

About that time, our server brought our meal. We really enjoyed the food, and we cleaned our plates. As I grossly sopped up the remains of my soft-shell crab with freshly buttered bread, I wondered if I would need a cardiac catheterization anytime soon.

We paid the bill, overtipped the server, and went to the car. Once I started the engine and turned on the lights, Mary Louise put her hand on my face, turned my cheek toward her, and gave me a deep kiss on the lips.

"Take me home, big boy, and don't speed. I don't want to ruin the mood by having to bail you out of jail." And I did just that.

CHAPTER 16

SURFSIDE FIRE DEPARTMENT

Saturday, September 7, 2002

We slept in, finally awakened by the screeching of the seagulls in search of food. We took our blend of Sumatra coffee on the main deck and enjoyed the morning's cool breeze. We finally got the energy to fry up some eggs and bacon, after which we fed Tip and walked him on the beach. He loved chasing the seagulls and didn't seem to mind it was a wasted effort. I couldn't imagine what he would do with a caught bird. Probably it would scare him to death. The walk must have been strenuous, as we three returned to our respective nap sites. Decadent.

We awoke around lunchtime and decided to go play nine holes of golf at the club and get a bite to eat there. Another Brady feeding accomplished, we teed off around 2 p.m. The weather was beautiful, with clear blue skies and a soft breeze. The water hazards were particularly thirsty that afternoon and rudely confiscated four of my newly purchased Pro V1 golf balls. Mary Louise, of course, deftly hit her little balls from hell down the middle every time, chipped onto the green, and buried the little gremlins into the cup, losing zero balls. Another loss for the golfing men of the Brady family, of which I was the only one.

We decided to have a cocktail on the club patio, which led to another burst of hunger, so we ordered a Caesar salad and split an order of fish and chips. Golfing, drinking, and eating finally done, we returned to the beach house. Tip was happy to see us and acted as though we had been gone for weeks.

Intent on staying up and enjoying the evening and each other's company, we showered, then promptly fell asleep in the king bed with the television on and the sliding doors open. I woke up about 3 a.m. due to a small flying-insect attack—mosquitoes—closed the doors, and fell immediately back to sleep. I dreamed of patenting perfect little golf balls that would hit the surface of the water and bounce directly onto the green. I remembered the dream well, flying around in my personal Gulfstream with the logo of a water-resistant "Brady ball" on the fuselage. Sadly, when awakened, I realized: a Gulfstream jet? Not now, not ever.

"Well, it's Sunday and already time to go home. This weekend time goes too fast," I declared to Mary Louise over orange-roasted coffee.

"What shall we do before the trip home? We still haven't discussed those papers, but there still is so much left for me to read. I think we'll have to make an appointment with each other to review the documents and discuss the implications."

"Well, I've been thinking about Uncle Howard and his desire to make amends, and I don't quite know where to go from here. You have any ideas?"

"Mrs. Jacoby told us that the man she called Mutt was picked up by the Surfside Fire Department. Why don't you call them this morning, go over there if need be, and see what you can discover?"

"Excellent idea. Want to come with me?"

"I'd prefer to leave the detecting to you and enjoy the deck and complete my review of Harold Sanders's will as it applies to you this morning. You can bring lunch home, as if we need any more food. I'll look after Tip."

I was anxious to find out what I could about the night of the alleged shooting, so I followed Mary Louise's advice and called. A fireman answered, and we spoke for a few minutes about what I was looking for. He seemed very cooperative and invited me to stop by the fire department in the next hour or so.

I made the thirty-mile drive back to Surfside Fire Station, which took about forty minutes. The building was a two-story structure, with two large red fire trucks parked in bays on the main level, one empty bay for an ambulance, and, I assumed, sleeping quarters on the second level. I was greeted by a young man who introduced himself as Lt. Jason Bowles.

"I'm Dr. Jim Bob Brady, from Houston. I'm an orthopedic surgeon there. My wife and I have a house in Indian Beach, and we're here for the weekend. I recently had a deathbed request from my uncle, Howard Peck, who many years ago was involved in some sort of shooting over at Kitty's. He didn't reveal the incident in great detail but said he wanted to make amends for what he thought might have been a murder."

"Sir, it sounds to me like you need to contact the authorities regarding this matter. This is beyond the scope of our fire department."

"Jason, that is my plan. Unfortunately my uncle died during liver-transplant surgery, and thus there is no more information to share, nor is there any action the police can take, now that he's passed on. However, my wife and I spoke to Evelyn Jacoby, who lives at Plainview Retirement Home and who said she was physically present when the shooting occurred."

"I know Miss Evelyn. She's the original owner of Kitty's."

"Well," I lied, "she implied you would be cooperative in showing me your records, because her memory is that one of your ambulances picked the wounded man up."

He stared at me for a long moment, obviously thinking he was making a career decision on whether to share his records with me or not. He sighed, and said, "Let's go take a look at what I have."

There was an office in back of the three bays, housing a desk, several chairs, and a fairly new desktop computer. "We've had only paper records here for years, but last year the chief wanted all our information converted to computer accessible. So he hired a lady to come in and do that. She completed the project a few months back, so you're in luck."

He typed some keys and called up a database of sorts. "When did this shooting occur?"

"I don't know for sure. Somewhere in the span of 1970 to 1975."

He looked at me like I had lost my mind. "Are you kidding? That's over twenty-five years ago!"

"Right. Can you access those records?"

He sighed again, heavier this time. "We don't get many shootings here, so I'm going to ask the computer to spit out any data regarding an ambulance pickup at Kitty's during that time frame. It'll take a few minutes."

While he stared at the screen and pecked at the keys, I wandered around the fire station. I always did like fire fighters and wondered what it would have been like to have that as a career. I was just about to climb aboard one of the trucks when Jason yelled to me.

"I've got something. Come look."

The screen showed one match for Jason's request. A white male, unknown name with no identification, was picked up in July of 1972 and transported somewhere we couldn't read.

"Where would you normally transport a gunshot victim?" I asked.

"Well, Freeport Hospital is seven miles, and Lake Jackson Hospital is ten miles, so they're the closest. The University of Texas Medical Branch in Galveston is forty miles, but that's a level-one facility. Generally, at least nowadays, we take the bad ones to UTMB, and the lesser injuries to one of the closer hospitals. I don't know for sure what they were doing back then, but it stands to reason the same policy existed."

"I can't read the computer abbreviation about where the unknown patient was transported."

"Well, Doc, there is a notation in the computer, which refers to more info on another screen. Let me see if I can . . . there it is. Want me to print it out?"

"That would be great."

As he hit the print icon and the printer whirred, I started to get a queasy feeling in the pit of my gut. I hoped it was a reaction from salad or seafood from the past couple of days. I wasn't sure I had it right, but if I did, it would be the mother of all coincidences.

He handed me the sheet of info. I read the printed version, while he stared at the monitor.

"It reads here that the victim was HAL. What does that mean?"

"As I remember, it stands for HOUSTON AIR LIFT."

"What's that?"

"Helicopter medivac to Houston."

"That makes no sense. Why would a shooting victim be airlifted to Houston when UTMB is just down the road?"

"That's the reason for the notation on a different screen. The file makes note of a separate incident going on at the same time as the shooting. You know UTMB is a state facility, and during the summer of 1972, there was nurses' strike in state-run Texas hospitals. It didn't apply to private or city-county hospitals. The notation read that all level-one trauma cases had to be sent to Houston, and I guess that the facilities in Houston that run the helicopter medivac provided a chopper to this part of the state during the strike. That's all I can figure, because a guy with a potentially fatal gunshot wound wouldn't have made it all the way there in an ambulance."

"I vaguely remember something about that nursing strike, but I was a first-year surgical resident. I had my own set of problems at the time. So, you're saying that this patient with a gunshot wound was flown to Houston in July of 1972 because of this nurses' strike?"

"Yes, sir, I believe that's correct."

"Does it say where he was taken?"

"No, sir. That's out of our jurisdiction."

"Any idea how to find out, Jason?"

"Well, I'd start with the medivac people."

"Thanks, Jason, you've been a tremendous help."

"No problem, sir. Let me know how it turns out."

CHAPTER 17

MEDICAL RECORDS

Sunday, September 8, 2002

A few years back, the University Medical Center Board of Governors had an epiphany. All medical records from the Med Center facilities should become paperless, which meant computerized. This was tremendous foresight on the board's part and preempted an eventual governmental mandate. It was a monumental task, considering that UMC was the largest medical complex in the world. The various medical centers encompassed five miles of land, employed over 100,000 people, including 20,000 physicians, and received 10 million patient encounters yearly. There were two medical schools, three nursing schools, a dental school, a pharmacy school, and seven specialty hospitals: orthopedics, cardiovascular, pediatrics, cancer, trauma, neurosurgery, and rehabilitation.

The file-digitalization project took several years and employed hundreds of data-entry personnel and coding specialists. When completed, the system was a beautiful thing, with physician and nursing access to all patients' medical records from any location in the complex. The board decided to begin the conversion with medical records from 1965. This was good, since I was looking for medical data from July 1972.

We had left Galveston early. I related my encounter with Jason the fireman to Mary Louise, which elevated my anxiety level by just discussing it with her.

"What do you think?" she asked, as we drove north on I-45 at a crawling speed of thirty miles an hour.

"I think I need to get to my office, log onto my computer, and access the three portals available to physicians and try and get more information."

"I totally understand. Drop Tip and me off at home and do what you need to do, sweetie. I finished reading the legal documents. We need to have a conversation. Frannie was right—this is a life-changing situation."

I arrived at my office, moved the paperwork debris to a chair, and fired up the computer. There were three portals available to physicians who were in the network. Privacy and piracy were an issue, so all physicians had to be identified by date of birth, thumbprint, and social security number, and had to be current in their respective board certifications. It was a process to be able to gain access to this impressive system, but once you were in, the tools it provided were invaluable to patient care.

The first portal was for physicians and their families' personal medical data. One could access office visits, lab work, and scans, and even compare colonoscopy results—with photos. Yippee.

The second portal allowed for patient-data access. If a patient presented to the ER with abdominal pain, the doctor could access data from any of the University hospitals on a computer as they examined the patient. Of course, the patient had to be conscious enough to provide their date of birth and social security number or have a family member present who could confirm that information. In the old days, we would have to order the patient's chart from medical records, only to discover that the patient had doctors in three locations in the UMC, and it would take hours, if not days, to be able to review critical information regarding the patient's medical history.

Now all this data was available at our fingertips, and we could provide immediate and accurate medical care with all parameters of the patient's medical history available.

The third portal was a little tricky, since that involved direct access to all medical records in all UMC hospitals. I was looking for an unconscious patient that had arrived via helicopter medivac from this area of southeast Texas at the University General ER, with no family and no identification, with a gunshot wound, in the first week of July 1972. I inserted all these parameters into the database and waited. The computer seemed to sleep for a while, then awakened and showed three possible matches on the screen.

I opened the first icon. The patient was female, brought in from the Beaumont, Texas, area, with a postpartum hemorrhage. It looked like the father of the baby was none too happy and decided to shoot the mother in the abdomen while she was in the hospital recovering from childbirth. I didn't bother to read the rest.

The second icon revealed a male, shot in the leg, transported from Sweeney, Texas, due to a massive bleed, probably from a severed femoral artery. In spite of the best efforts of the helicopter crew and the ER staff, the man expired upon arrival.

The third icon showed a male, shot in the chest, transported in from Galveston County via HAL on July 1, 1972. He was unconscious, with no family and no identification. He was treated in the ER, transferred to the operating room where he had surgery, then admitted to the hospital from there. There was no more data regarding his outcome. I scrolled down the ER intake form to the last line, where the physician in charge had to sign off on the treatment. I knew the name all too well:

James Robert Brady, MD.

The memorable patient from my first day in the ER, the Mutt that Evelyn described from the shooting at Kitty's, and my uncle's friend Bull from his railroad days, were one and the same.

CHAPTER 18

THE WILL

Sunday, September 8, 2002

Iinformed Mary Louise of my findings on the car phone on the way home. She was uncharacteristically quiet when I arrived, suggesting we have a martini at home and order in Chinese food from Shanghai River Restaurant. That sounded like a reasonable plan to me. I had an early call for Monday surgery and hoped to be in bed by 9 p.m. I didn't want the Pandora's box that my Uncle Howard had opened to be discussed any further. I was, however, most interested in Mary Louise's assessment of Harold Sanders's will as it applied to us.

"You remember that my father was a geologist?"

"I do."

"And he wanted me to follow in his footsteps, so in deference to him, I took a couple of geology courses at SMU. To his dismay, fashion and marketing was my 'thing,' so a degree in geology didn't pan out for me. But for years, I would hear him talking business on the phone and at dinner parties at the house, and as a result, I picked up on many terms having to do with oil and gas exploration and production.

"Dad died way too young from cigarette smoking, one of the many reasons I'm glad you finally quit last year. As a little girl, he would talk to me about deals he was putting together for the company, and I would see the excitement in his eyes about new discoveries of oil and gas fields. He was a huge proponent of the United States becoming energy self-sufficient. Geologic exploration was his life.

"With that in mind, I can summarize what this codicil to Harold Sanders's will states and can explain with some surety what it means to you and me. Are you with me so far?"

"Absolutely. What I'm wondering is—"

"Jim Bob, why don't you wait until I've given you my version of Mr. O'Leary's facts, and then see what questions you might have, okay baby?"

"Of course. Please proceed—and may I say I love it when you call me baby."

She smiled. "Do you know where Cotulla, Texas, is?"

"Somewhere in South Texas. I went on a quail hunt down there a long time ago."

"It's in La Salle County, south of San Antonio. That area is known for two things: dove and quail hunting, and oil and gas production. My father spent a lot of time down there for work and used to tell stories about the early days of oil and gas drilling, before the blowout preventer was invented. A blowout was when the drill bit reached the desired formation and struck hydrocarbons, causing a literal explosion of oil and gas, wasting hundreds, maybe thousands of gallons of oil, pushed out by the natural gas. If you've ever seen the movie *Giant*, you know what I'm talking about, albeit fictionalized.

"The Sanders family has been down there for years, having started buying up land back in the late 1800s. Every generation has expanded the Double Eagle Ranch, and at last count they own 25,000 acres with the mineral rights. Some time ago, a variety of large and small oil companies started leasing land and drilling test wells. It turns out there is a lot of oil and natural gas under their land. The Sanders are ranchers, of course, and run hundreds of cattle on their property, but realistically, their income is derived from petroleum production.

"When Harold Sanders died, for whatever reason, he decided to deed you 100 acres of his ranchland. His wife supported the gift, so you must have really put a spell on those folks during your treatment," she said, laughing. "Just teasing, sweetie, but I couldn't resist. At any rate, that 100 acres was part of ranchland leased by Texaco originally, but their geologists couldn't justify drilling there because the oil and gas was not close to the surface and was embedded in what is called 'shale rock.'

"When the will was originally read, the three Sanders children opposed his gift to you on general principles, stating that Mr. Sanders's head was cloudy from infection in his body, antibiotics, and general malaise, to the extent he didn't know what he was doing. Mrs. Sanders signed off on the codicil, so I don't quite understand what the kids thought *her* 'mental incapacity' was at the time, but nonetheless, the dispensation of the will proceeds was halted by the contesting of the will.

"The kids, however, wanted their money, so the lawyers went back and forth for a while, agreed to terms, and everything in the will was eventually resolved except for your little 100 acres of land. You were never notified of your gift because of the will being contested, probably a mistake on the lawyers' part, but that's why you're just now finding this out."

She sipped a little water and continued.

"What has essentially triggered this codicil coming to light now is fracking. Know what that is?"

"Not really, although I've heard the term."

"It's been around a while but recently has changed the face of oil and gas production. Fracking is a process of injecting liquid—water, sand, and chemicals—at high pressures into shale rock to force open existing fissures in order to extract oil and gas. There has been controversy about whether or not this process could contaminate ground water, but fracking has continued, nonetheless. The Sanders family was making a considerable amount of money from royalties on oil and gas production, but fracking has allowed hydrocarbon forma-tions that once were unable to be accessed to now be extracted, and with it has brought a significant increase in revenue to the Double Eagle Ranch."

"The rich get richer, they say," I interjected.

"Yes, they do, and sometimes the not-so-rich benefit. Turns out your little 100 acres is right in the middle of the shale-fracking proj-ect, much to the dismay of the family and the oil companies that have interests in the property. There is no line drawn in the sand, so drilling has continued on the property with no regard to a boundary between 'your' land and the rest of the Sanders property. So now the production is comingled and has been for a couple of years. Turns out that the Sanders family will have to pay you off for past production and future production royalties in order to get you out of the picture so they can continue to explore and produce more wells and make even more money."

"Wow, royalty interests sound good. What kind of money are they talking about? Maybe I can get a new car."

"Oil and gas prices fluctuate with the market, and both are trad-ed as commodities and futures. According to Mr. O'Leary's figures, oil alone has been down to twenty-eight dollars per barrel and up to thirty-seven dollars per barrel the past year, from 2001 to 2002, so the amount of money we're discussing varies from day to day. Also, remember there are now two existing oil and gas wells on that 100 acres, producing a total of 1300 barrels of oil and 400 mcf—that's thousand cubic feet—of natural gas per day. Royalty interests are cal-culated at 15 percent, and although you're not family, as the sole owner of that 100 acres, you're a royalty owner. A conservative esti-mate of your revenue would be to multiply an average current price of oil at thirty dollars per barrel and gas at five dollars per mcf times the production.

"Mr. O'Leary does point out that these various numbers we're talking about may or may not be completely accurate, but represent, in his opinion, 'precision guesswork.' I think that's pretty funny."

Mary Louise pulled a small calculator out of her purse and started to enter numbers. "I'm glad you're sitting down, Jim Bob. The total revenue from the two wells is $41,000 . . . per day. As a 15-percent royalty owner, your portion would be $6,150 per day, which is $184,000 per month, or $2,214,000 per year. The average well life in that part of Texas is twenty years, which would be a total revenue of $44,280,000 before taxes, if it were not for the gradual decline in production over time. Declines are calculated either as a linear decline or a hyperbolic curve decline, depending on the formation and the type of well drilled. This decline has been calculated over twenty years, and the petroleum engineers have estimated that your royalty interest with the decline factored in would generate $26,937,414.

"But don't forget that oil and gas revenue is taxed at ordinary income levels, which in our case is 39.6 percent. A lot of people feel hydrocarbon revenue should be taxed at capital-gains levels, which is lower, but that is not currently the case. Bottom line, after taxes, your share would be $16,162,448. The Sanders family is willing to pay the taxes and any expenses associated with engineering calculations and pay you up front, regardless of the future of the wells. Mr. O'Leary has brought you a buyout offer of $16,500,000."

I was speechless. Finally, I sputtered, "You mean a cash offer? Now, all at once? Of 16 million dollars???"

"Yes, my dear. You would have to sign a waiver stating that, despite future drilling and future oil and gas prices, you accept that sum for now and all time and would not renege on the offer at some future point in time, regardless of what circumstances you might find yourself in. You would be a wealthy man and could do whatever you want—except get rid of me."

CHAPTER 19

M&M

Monday, September 9, 2002

I'm not sure I slept that night. I was giddy, I was afraid, I cried. Mary Louise was up with me part of the time, not speaking, just holding me. I must have finally dozed off, because the alarm woke me at 5 a.m. I got a cup of coffee, looked to see that Tip was still snuggled up next to the mistress of the house, and headed to the hospital.

Both Tim and Shelley had enjoyed a weekend off, so they were in good moods. Four cases were scheduled: two virgin knee replacements, and two redo hip replacements. Shelley was tired of what she called the "easy duty" in the virgin prosthesis OR and opted to help me in the redo hip room. Tim and I breezed through the knee procedures in record time and it was a good thing, because we got hung up on one of the redo hips. The patient had an osteoporosis condition—soft bone disease—and we had to be extraordinarily careful. In spite of that, during the process where an electric reamer is used to remove old cement and is run down the shaft of the femur—thigh bone—we heard a *crack*. I called in x-ray, and the films showed that there was a spiral fracture about midshaft, well below where the tip of the new prosthesis would end up. The nursing supervisor had to call the implant manufacturer and bring over an extended-stem prosthesis, one that would extend below the fracture site. Then, to reinforce the new stem, we had to put in cerclage wires around the femoral shaft, not unlike using barbed wire on a ranch fence post. Mechanic, carpenter, and cowboy; all in a day's work for Dr. Jim Bob Brady.

And suddenly I was going to be worth a lot of money that I didn't have to work for, and it wasn't sitting well with me. I wanted to head home and discuss my feelings with Mary Louise. She understood me better than I did.

I dictated my operative reports, talked to the families, and schmoozed the nurses in the recovery room. Walking back to my locker to change, Fran called.

"All okay there?"

"Yep. Mostly good day. What's happening?"

"You're invited to the weekly M&M conference. Starts at four thirty."

"You mean today? Man, I'm bushed. Why did the committee invite me?"

"Because your Uncle Howard is the first patient they are discussing."

"Really? Wonder why?"

"Uh, I would think because a liver-transplant patient died in the operating room. I don't think that sits well with the powers that be."

"Hmm. I guess you're right. What time is it now?"

"Four fifteen."

"Great. All right, I'll go."

"Rae and I are leaving at five, so we'll see your cheery face bright and early for clinic in the morning. Did you ever call that lawyer about the personal matter?"

"I did. I'll tell you about it later. Safe drive home."

M&M conferences—morbidity and mortality—were recurring conferences held by medical and surgical services at most large academic medical centers. The focus of the conference was not on blame but rather on education and quality improvement. At UMC, they took place every Monday afternoon. Normally, the chief resident on the service gave a presentation about a particular case, and on occasion the attending physician or surgeon made comments regarding their treatment of the patient in question. Most of the cases involved surgical complications and deaths. After thinking about it, I could see why Uncle Howard's case was being presented.

I headed over to the Bowen Memorial Amphitheater and arrived just in time for the beginning. The moderator was the chief of surgery, Dr. Bradshaw.

"First case up today is Howard Peck. He was an uncle of Dr. James Brady, whom I've invited here today. Thanks for coming, Jim. The chief resident on Dr. Crawford's service will present the case."

"Good afternoon. Howard Peck was a seventy-two-year-old Methodist minister from Jasper, Texas. He had long-standing cirrhosis of the liver, secondary to alcoholism in his younger days. He developed an episode of hepatic failure and was treated at East Texas Medical Center. Consideration was given for a possible liver transplant. He underwent a workup there and was discovered to have a hepatoma, a carcinoma of the liver and not an uncommon finding in a cirrhotic liver. He was then transferred here to the care of Dr. Damon, chief of oncology, who initiated an extensive workup, including a liver biopsy. Mr. Peck was confirmed to have advanced cirrhosis and concomitant carcinoma of the liver, but without metastases. Without systemic spread, he was a candidate for transplant. His family was tested for compatibility, and his son Rico was a perfect match. He consented to be the donor, and Dr. Crawford was selected to perform the surgery.

"The procedure took place last Wednesday and was routine until it wasn't. We had detached the old cirrhotic liver and clamped the major vessels and the hepatic duct, and we were waiting for the donor liver to arrive. Once that occurred, we began the suturing process of attaching the new liver to the patient's vessels and ducts. Suddenly, blood arose in the wound to the extent that none of the anatomy was visible. We suctioned extensively, transfused the patient, gave him clotting factors, and ultimately called a code blue to bring in advisors from the medical service, all to no avail. Mr. Peck was pronounced dead in the operating room.

"Permission for a post was obtained from the family. The cause of death was bleeding from a near-necrosis of a section of the head of the pancreas. On microscopic examination, this area contained an adenocarcinoma of the pancreas. The cancer was either disturbed by the manipulations going on in the abdomen during the liver transplant, or perhaps was affected by a reduction of blood flow to the area as a consequence of the anesthesia and surgery itself.

"I obtained the preoperative CT, MRI, and PET scans and reviewed all the films with two of my colleagues: the radiologist that interpreted the films, and Dr. Jeff Clarke, assistant chief of pathology, who performed the autopsy. None of us could identify the pancreatic lesion on any of the films.

"In summary, we feel this is a hemorrhagic death during a liver-transplant procedure due to a concomitant pancreatic cancer that was unrecognized prior to surgery. In retrospect, we do not see how this situation could have been prevented. Thank you."

Dr. Bradshaw asked for any questions from the audience. There were none. Whether the attending physicians' politeness was in honor of my being present for the conference, or simply that no one had any questions, I didn't know. I thought the chief resident presented a clear and concise recitation of the case. Hopefully this would squelch any further discussion of a lawsuit by my mother and Howard's immediate family.

I decided, in fact, to stop by Rico Peck's room on the way out, provided he was still in the hospital. I felt I had neglected the family in the process of taking care of my own business, so extending them an olive branch by making an appearance after the M&M conference seemed a wise move.

I wandered through the seemingly endless hallways and finally arrived at the elevator bank that led up to the transplant ward.

Once on the eighth floor, I stopped at the nursing station to confirm Rico Peck's room number and his continued presence in the hospital. Nurse Rita Walker greeted me.

"Dr. Brady, so nice to see you, and let me say on behalf of all the staff here that we are so sorry about the death of Mr. Peck. Tragic, just tragic."

"Thanks much. I just returned from the M&M conference, and it was clear to me that his demise was no fault of the hospital or the treating physicians. My uncle had an undiagnosed pancreatic cancer, not seen on any preoperative studies, which caused an unstoppable bleed during the surgery. A tragedy, yes, but not preventable. I came by to visit with my aunt and cousins, if they are still here, and let them know the findings of the committee."

Rita Walker looked a little uncomfortable, and said, "You haven't heard?"

"I guess not. What?"

"The family checked Rico Peck out yesterday. The mother, wife of the deceased, demanded a release from Dr. Damon. He consented, provided the patient stay nearby in the Marriott. They have been carefully watching him for bleeding, the most common complication after a portion of the liver is used for a transplant."

"That doesn't sound good. Any talk of a lawsuit?"

"Not that I heard while they were here. However, yesterday one of the nurses on the day shift overhead Mrs. Peck on the phone, speaking words about the hospital that were none too kind. In fact, she told me that the Pecks had a visitor later in the morning, a man dressed in a very expensive three-piece suit. The nurse swore to me it was one of those lawyers that advertise on television."

CHAPTER 20

DEWEY MOSS

Monday, September 9, 2002

I phoned Mary Louise from the car, but the call went to voice mail. When I arrived at home, I found a note on the kitchen counter.

Jim Bob, with all that you're dealing with, I feel certain you forgot about the March of Dimes board dinner meeting. I should be home by eight thirty. I picked up some food from the Grotto for you, pasta and salad, so heat up the pasta with some olive oil and have a drink. Monday Night Football is on, and your former Oilers, now the Tennessee Titans, are playing the New England Patriots. And I know how you love to root against Bud Adams and our former team.

Relax! Tip has been fed.

M. L.

Since it was fall and football season, I avoided my usual martini and went for the big gun: Macallan eighteen-year-old scotch. Silly, I know, but while I love martinis in the summer months, I must have single-malt scotch starting in the fall, or at least while watching fall sports. It was now officially that time. The behavior was probably caused by a leftover genetic particle from my Scottish and Irish ancestry, but I was never sad about it.

I greeted Tip, rubbed his ears, spoke to him in doggie baby talk, then showered, turned on the TV, sipped some scotch, and watched the Patriots begin to dismantle the Titans' defense. "Crush 'em like a bug, Brady!" I yelled repeatedly. At some point in time I fell asleep and woke up during halftime, and then only because of the volume of laughter coming from John Madden during the halftime report. I jumped up and nuked the pasta with olive oil, as ordered. I enjoyed my caprese salad first, then the pappardelle pasta with thick chunks of tender chicken. Food fit for a king—or a rich guy from oil production that he didn't bother to work for.

I of course couldn't let anything go. I worried about my aunt filing a lawsuit against University Hospital. I didn't think she had a leg to stand on, but the lawyers these days could bring a case against Mother Theresa and make her sound like Lizzie Borden. Sometimes those cases were settled for large sums just to avoid publicity and embarrassment for the parties concerned.

And then I worried about Mutt, a.k.a. Bull. What happened to him? Was he alive? The medical records I reviewed ended with his transfer up to surgery at University General. There would have to be more information available. Tomorrow, time permitting, I would call or make a trip to the medical records department for University General Hospital and see what I could find out. But tomorrow was a clinic day, and I was usually seeing patients until 3 or 4 p.m., after which I was usually so tired, I could barely dictate charts.

My thoughts then turned to all that money that was just waiting to be signed for. I needed to discuss that with Mary Louise again, and I needed to set up another meeting with Tom O'Leary. M. L. would have to participate.

Those thoughts continued to swim around in my brain until I once again fell asleep in my lounge chair. I dreamed of lawyers in chain mail using long sharp swords to lacerate the arms and legs of doctors in white coats. I felt I was being pushed up against a wall and thought maybe they were after me, but finally I awoke, startled to see Mary Louise escorting me to the bedroom.

"You must have fallen asleep, Jim Bob. You always clean your plates and wash your glass. The dirty dishes frightened me. Are you okay? Help me get you into bed."

"You bet. Just tired. Glad to see you. I don't think I walked Tip."

"I know. He told me."

"What, we have a talking dog now? I just can't take any more."

And with that said, I fell onto the covers and dreamed of Lela Belle Peck driving around a small dusty town in East Texas in a new Rolls-Royce.

Five in the morning came early on Tuesday. I showered, got coffee, and went to work. Rounds went smoothly. The patient with the difficult hip redo replacement was fortunately doing well. A nice-looking middle-aged woman was sitting in a recliner next to the bed, watching the patient sleep.

"I hear Mama gave you a little trouble yesterday, Dr. Brady."

"Oh, she was no trouble, but that hip sure was. You heard what happened?"

"Yes, my sister told me. We're taking turns with the opportunity to help out our mama. She's done so much for us all our lives, it's a joy to be able to give back."

Wow. What a great thing that was to say. I didn't see that happening with my dear sweet mother, Lucille Brady.

"The healing will be a little slower, but she's a tough lady. She'll be fine," I said, as I smiled and nodded to the visitor.

Rounds were otherwise uneventful, and I made it to the office by 7 a.m. Being Tuesday, there were problems from the weekend that had to be seen and taken care of. And while they were mostly minor issues, they were still time consuming. I didn't finish seeing patients until 4:30 p.m.

"Pop, you going to make it?" Fran asked.

"Yes, but much wearier than I used to be. Nobody told me this was how I would feel coming up on sixty."

"Don't even think about seventy, then," echoed Rae.

"You ladies headed home?"

"Just about. Anything else you need?"

"Could you get Dr. Dewey Moss on the phone please?"

"Sure thing. See you tomorrow."

Fran buzzed me when Dewey answered. "Hey, Dew, how's it going, old friend?"

"Jim Bob, if life was any better, I couldn't stand it. I'm headed over to do a bowel obstruction. There are all kinds of dead intestines in there, I'm sure. Can't wait."

"Gross. I can't think of anything worse."

"You bone docs. Y'all like everything all clean and neat, no blood, and fracture ends that fit together perfectly. Give me a shotgun wound to the abdomen, with multiple holes in the small and large bowel. Nothing better."

"Dewey, please stop. I won't be able to eat dinner tonight. I have two things to discuss with you. First, Princess Sara and her appendectomy. How is she healing and when can I replace her hip?"

"Princess Sara. Brady, I'm in love. I think I'll let her take me back to the kingdom and live happily ever after."

"Dew, what about Erik?"

"You mean the husband? I'm not worried about him. He's a wuss."

"Dew, you've seen a picture of the famous Tamborinian ceremonial axe, right? That giant, extremely heavy and sharp-looking axe? Just saying."

"Brady, you're ruining the moment for me. A man can always dream."

"Dream about your wife and kids. Now when can I do the hip?"

"What's your next operating day?"

"Tomorrow, Wednesday."

"Too soon. Friday or Monday?"

"Monday it is. Second thing, do you remember that patient from 1972? THE patient?"

"Brady, why are you still obsessing about that guy? That was thirty years ago."

I briefly told him the story of Uncle Howard and his request to make amends, and my involvement with the man in the ER. "My question is, did the guy make it after you repaired his pulmonary artery? I'm ashamed to say that I was so busy in the ER with that twenty-four-hours-on and twenty-four-hours-off schedule that I just forgot about him. Over the following twenty-four hours I probably treated another fifty patients, maybe a hundred. I mean, what kind of shitty doctor forgets about that kind of experience with a patient? And I never even knew his name!"

"Brady, don't beat yourself up. That was residency. This is the real world, and that was not. That was a sleep-deprived, five-year-long fog. We're all lucky to have survived, must less to have remembered all the patients that we treated. And by the way, the guy lived and was eventually discharged from the hospital, best I can remember. I know for sure he lived long enough to get his sutures removed. After that, I can't tell you. Check with medical records at University General. They can give you more info. And if makes you feel any better, I don't remember his name either. He was just another gunshot-wound victim we saved. Nice talking to you, but I gotta run. The bowels are calling."

CHAPTER 21

MEDICAL RECORDS

Tuesday, September 10, 2002

I decided to place a call to medical records at University General Hospital before I made a trip over there. While theoretically that facility was under the auspices of University Medical Center, the staff and employees there tended to be a little territorial. In the past, on occasion, when I needed some information regarding a patient that had been transferred from General to the orthopedic service at UMC, they were less than forthcoming with the medical records. I saw no reason why this should be, but neither did I understand the reasons for world hunger or genocide, or why some schmo from Waco would inherit a bunch of oil-production money. Some issues were beyond understanding at my pay grade.

"Medical records, Natalie speaking."

"Hello, Natalie, this is Dr. James Brady calling. I need some information about a patient."

I gave her my global physician ID number, as well as my office address, office number, and my Texas medical license number. I almost volunteered my underwear size but thought better of it.

"Okay, Doc, I've verified that you're who you say you are. What can I do for you?"

I gave her an abbreviated version of Uncle Howard's exploits with Bull, as well as confirmation of the shooting of Mutt by his companion, according to Mrs. Jacoby, former owner of Kitty's. Then I linked that information with the facts of my having treated said patient in the emergency room, and the date of July 1, 1972.

"Sir, I don't see the problem here."

"Well, I need the patient's name, Natalie."

"You mean to tell me your uncle shot this man, and a diner owner witnessed the shooting, and you operated on the victim, and none of you knew this patient's name? How can that be?"

"It was the seventies?"

"Doc, I hope that if I get shot, and someone witnesses it, and I get flown into this hospital in a helicopter, and get operated on, that someone will sure as hell remember my name!"

I could hear the computer keys clicking in the background, as I patiently waited. Having a drink seemed like a very good idea at the moment, but I was afraid Natalie from medical records could hear the ice clinking and would decide not to help me. So, I poured Glenlivet twelve-year scotch into a glass, straight up.

"Lester Rollo Mimms."

"What? You found it?"

"Yep. That's why they pay me the big bucks, like not."

"Do you have any other info on him, like an address, phone number, date of birth, social security number, residence at the time?"

"I've got his personals from July of 1972. I can't say that it's still current. I've looked through the records, and he had a repair of the pulmonary artery, was here for two weeks, then discharged after his sutures were removed. I don't have any records that indicate he ever returned."

She gave me his address in Oklahoma City back in 1972, and his phone number at the time. She also reluctantly provided me with his date of birth and social security number, worried she somehow might get into trouble with the HIPAA people. I told her that my lips were sealed from federal busybodies and that I would forget her name in order to protect her identity after our conversation ended.

"Don't you dare forget my name, Dr. Brady! Although it seems to me you and your colleagues are pretty good at that." And then she hung up.

Touché.

I dragged my weary self home. Mary Louise fixed me a scotch, and I gave her my rendition of the day's events. Tip wedged his snout between my legs as I sat at a barstool at the kitchen island. I gave him my two-handed facial and body rubdown, after which he went to the corner and fell immediately asleep on his pillow.

Mary Louise served pot roast, my favorite, so I could enjoy a relaxed meal at home.

"Well, you now have his name, after all these years. How does it feel?"

"Strange. Lester Rollo Mimms. I keep repeating his name; for what reason, I don't know. Unless I'm somehow afraid I'll forget it."

"I think you have done an amazing job of discovering the man's identity. You've done all the hard work. Why don't you give J. J. a call and let him run with the info you have? He's got all the tools. Besides, it should be easy, now that you have Mr. Mimms's date of birth and social security number."

"Sounds like a great plan. I barely have enough energy to take care of my own business, much less continuing this research for my deceased Uncle Howard. The matter of the oil inheritance is also weighing heavily on my mind. I feel as though I don't deserve it. I've always worked hard for what I have. Laying what I think is a fortune in my lap with no effort whatsoever on my part seems almost like stealing."

"Don't be silly. You've dedicated the majority of your life to helping people, whether you got paid for it or not. You are one of the most respected docs around these parts, and you have earned that respect through a ton of education and a workload most people would collapse under. So don't tell me you are not deserving. This is a cosmic reward, Jim Bob, and you should accept it graciously, and do something with it that benefits not only yourself, but others. You have the opportunity of a lifetime, one that most people can only dream about. I'll be happy to help you figure out what to do, but never, ever say to me you are not deserving."

I pondered those words but said nothing. What was there to say?

"Now that you've had a few sips of your drink, I will tell you that your mother called today."

"And?"

"Howard's funeral is this Friday at 1 p.m."

"And we have to attend, right?"

"Most certainly."

"Where will it be?"

"Jasper, Texas."

"That's what, a two-and-a-half-hour drive each way? Think we can do a round trip, or should we spend the night?"

"I've already booked a room for us."

"Sounds like you have it under control, M. L. Any other news?"

"Well, you won't like it, and neither did I, but your mother gave me another tidbit of information. Would you like to hear it now or after dinner?"

"Now, please."

"Your Aunt Lela is going to sue the hospital, and all the doctors that treated Howard, for medical negligence."

CHAPTER 22

LESTER ROLLO MIMMS

Wednesday, September 11, 2002

Wednesday's scheduled caseload started out reasonably light, two virgin hip replacements and two virgin knee replacements. However, I had been on call the night before, a duty that occurred every fifth night. There were four other surgeons in the group that did the same kind of work that I did, so we rotated call. Tim Stacy, the fellow, had called me twice during the evening, informing me of two admissions, each for a fractured hip, and I told him to make them NPO (nothing by mouth) and put them on today's schedule if they were medically cleared. I had minimal recollection of the phone calls, since he woke me from a dead sleep twice, but far be it from me to tell the house staff that. A surgeon prides himself on being instantly alert when awakened from a dead sleep, but trust me, that fades with age.

So, after six major orthopedic procedures, and standing in the OR for about ten hours, I was spent. I managed to make a pass through the recovery room to check on the last few postoperative patients. I spoke to the relatives still in the waiting room. I wandered upstairs to the orthopedic floor and checked in on the remainder of the post-ops. The patients were all doing well, and just as important-ly, the families were okay and seemingly happy.

I stopped by my office and checked for any urgencies on my desk. Fran and Rae had left earlier but didn't fail to add a couple of pounds of paperwork to my desk. I made a few required calls but ignored the mass of debris, the purpose of which was primarily to make me aware of the denial of permission for surgical treatment for my patients without "further information." And of course, I would need to disclose this "further information" to an insurance-company clerk with no medical training whatsoever. Oh boy, what fun. Would it be so wrong to wish those insurance people to be infected with leprosy?

I made it home without wrecking the truck and literally stumbled out of the elevator that led to our apartment. Mary Louise had the door open when I arrived, drink in hand.

"For me?" I asked.

"Yes, my darling. We're dining in, and J. J. has joined us."

I kissed my wife, hugged my son, and collapsed into a recliner. Tip sensed my weariness, walked over, and laid his big fat head in my lap.

"Long day, Pop?" asked J. J.

"Yep. I'm getting too old for this intense of a schedule. I need to rethink my life."

"Well, relax and let me tell you all about Lester Rollo Mimms."

"How did you know—"

"Mom called, said you needed help, and help is here. No charge, by the way." Ironic that I could now afford his services if I took the payout . . .

"Lester Rollo Mimms was born in the summer of 1929 in Edmond, Oklahoma. His father worked for the Missouri-Kansas-Texas Railroad Company, known affectionately as the 'Katy.' Mimms went to high school in Edmond, graduated in 1947, and enlisted in the army. This was two years after World War II ended, and four years before the Korean War began, so he was a 'tweener.' He was sent to Fort Jackson, South Carolina, which had become a replacement training center for new soldiers and mobilized National Guards after WWII. The Fifth Infantry Division was reactivated as a training division as well, so Mimms became a part of Fifth Infantry.

"He apparently impressed the brass; he was promoted quickly from private to corporal to sergeant. As a non-commissioned officer—an NCO—he obtained his position of authority by promotion through the enlisted ranks, since he had not attended a military academy and did not have a college degree. He achieved the rank of Master Sergeant and was primarily involved in the training of new recruits.

"He could have stayed in for twenty years and probably made the rank of Sergeant Major and would have been the recipient of a decent pension, but he resigned after ten years of service, in 1957. The records show he was involved in some sort of event at that time, but the documents I reviewed had been partially redacted. I was unable to determine what occurred, but he was honorably discharged, so it couldn't have been too bad. Mimms returned to Edmond, Oklahoma, and went to work for the Katy at age twenty-eight. He stayed in Edmond for five years, then moved to Fort Worth, Texas, in 1962, still with the Katy Railroad. He's been there since. He retired in 1994 at age 65.

"He owns a small home in a section of Fort Worth called Arlington Heights, off Camp Bowie Blvd. He has minimal credit-card debt and apparently lives frugally and off the radar. No tickets, no arrests, and no lawsuits against him. Pretty much what I would expect from a former military man. Also, there is no record of him ever being married or having children."

"Man, that is an incredible amount of information on Mr. Mimms. I can't believe you came up with all that in one day."

"Modern technology, Pops. There is no longer any privacy."

"In my last and only conversation with Howard Peck, he called himself 'Preacher,' and Mr. Mimms 'Bull.' There was something about him being railroad police?"

"He was a union man, as most railroad employees are, and it's simply amazing how much data you can learn about a person from union records. Mimms was a member of the Brotherhood of Railroad Trainmen until that union merged with three others to form the Transportation Union in 1969. The Katy Railroad essentially disappeared in 1989, as it was merged into the Union Pacific Railroad. Mimms continued in the union as a Union Pacific employee until he retired.

"He started out as a switchman, whose job it is to operate switches on the railroad tracks and to assist in moving cars in the railway yard. He was a pretty smart man and quickly mastered that job. He was then promoted to yardmaster, whose job is to be in charge of the railyard. That job is stressful and requires some smarts and patience. The yardmaster manages and coordinates all activities in the yard, including rolling livestock into trains, breaking down trains into individual railroad cars, and switching trains from track to track in the yard.

"From what I gleaned in the union records, Mimms was working as a yardmaster in Edmond and continued in that capacity when he moved to Fort Worth. At some point in time after moving, however, he became a railroad police officer, or "bull." The modern-day railroad police officer primarily spends their time investigating crimes, such as thieves breaking into freight cars and trailers. They do spend some of their time removing trespassers off the trains, such as travelers formerly known as 'hobos,' and these days, Mexican nationals after they have crossed the border illegally. In the old days the rail police were called "bulls" due to their fierceness and willingness to do anything to get the trespassers removed.

"Mimms became a railroad police officer in 1966 and maintained that position until 1972, the year he was allegedly shot by your Uncle Howard. There was a gap in his pay stubs in the union records for about two months, which would correspond to time off for recovery from the gunshot wound. Apparently, he was a very valuable employee, because I found no repercussions from his work absence. The only unusual item I found was that Mimms was allowed to be a railroad police officer in a sort of 'traveling' role. He performed his duties not only in the railroad yard in Fort Worth but in railroad yards from Oklahoma City all the way down to Galveston. He was on the road all the time. I didn't find any other employees in the union with that sort of job description."

"Well, Uncle Howard told me they used to ride the rails together, but that meant that Mimms, or Bull, rode as a railroad cop, and my uncle rode as a trespasser.

"Listen, son, I appreciate all the work you've done here. I don't know how to thank you, except to say that I'm beat and headed for the sack and will leave you alone with your favorite parent."

"Thanks, Pop. Listen, I know you're tired, so I'll leave the dossier on Howard Peck with Mom. You can review it at your leisure and call me with questions."

CHAPTER 23

HOWARD PECK

Thursday, September 12, 2002

Mary Louise had to beat on my shoulder to get me up Thursday morning. I was five minutes late for rounds, but no one commented. Rounds went smoothly, and I was able to convince a few folks to leave the hospital, some to their respective homes, but most to the rehab unit.

I made a special side trip to the VIP wing to see Princess Sara, to assess her progress and to inform her that I would be replacing her hip on Monday. I went to the nurses' station first and, armed with the floor nurse and the charge nurse, we stepped across the hall and encountered the two bodyguards.

"Morning, gents, I need to see Princess Sara."

They stared at me, then at each other, and spoke in what I would assume was Tamborinian, and stepped aside.

The room was enormous enough to be considered a suite, with a hospital bed and bathroom on one side and a sitting area with a pullout sofa on the other.

"There is room for all your family here, Sara, and a couple of distant cousins," I said.

"Dr. Brady, I heard you coming down the hall."

"Was I talking too loud?"

"No. I heard your boots clicking on the tile."

"Oh. I left my horse at the elevator, ma'am."

She giggled.

"Doc Moss has cleared you to have your hip replaced on Monday. You still good with that?"

"Yes. It's been killing me lying in this bed. I keep turning from side to side, but it continues to ache all the time. I am ready, Doctor."

"Well, I'll put you in early Monday morning, so get a good night's sleep on Sunday."

"Thank you, Doctor, and I should say the same to you."

Clinic came and went. It seemed to me that Thursday office hours were better than Tuesday hours. That was probably because my brain was telling me that I had the next three days off, and by releasing whatever endorphins were necessary to improve my mood, I actually experienced a mood elevation. I didn't remember all the physiology from medical school, but better living through chemistry was my motto.

I cleaned off my desk, like a good little surgeon. I even called a couple of those nitwits from the insurance company, baffled them with some good ol' Texas bullshit, and received approval to repair my patients' orthopedic problems. The two surgeries were each postponed a month due to the insurance company's delay tactics. Seriously? And what for? To control the surgeon and the hospital? Possibly just to enhance their bottom line? If an insurance company delays a thousand surgeries across the country for a month, or two, even, how much money in investment interest would the companies gain? Nope, the future of medicine was not bright, in my humble opinion.

Mary Louise was packing when I arrived home. I poured myself some Macallan 18, added one ice cube, and sipped the nectar of the gods.

"Jim Bob, do you want me to pack for you? And don't hem and haw around and say you're going to do it, and then it gets to be nine or ten at night, and I end up doing it for you anyway. This is your only chance, my very precious."

"Yes, please. I'm just too tired."

"Good choice, my man. Make yourself a leftover roast beef sandwich if you're hungry." She kissed me on the lips and gave me a butt pat. Her tube top and matching shorts were beyond fetching. And her aroma—she smelled of gladiolas.

"You have that look, young man."

"I have that feeling, too."

She removed her suitcase and a hanging bag from the bed, turned down the covers, and crawled into bed. "I thought you said you were too tired to pack."

"I am. There is only one part of my anatomy that can move at this moment."

"Oh, I see. Well, since you're so tired, why don't you just let me do all the work."

And she did.

I woke up starving. It was 11 p.m. Mary Louise was sound asleep, purring like our now-deceased Cat used to. I padded into the kitchen and made myself a cold roast beef sandwich on white toast with lots of mayo and a dill pickle. I poured a glass of milk and started to read what J. J. called his dossier on Howard Peck. I felt certain I would know a good deal about the information in the report because Howard was, after all, my uncle, brother of my mother, Lucille Brady. And I hoped I would find some classic J. J. ad libs.

Dad, he wrote, *Howard was born in 1930, at home, in Zavalla, Texas. He was the youngest of nine children, with eight sisters. He was precocious and a good-looking kid. His sisters doted on him and did everything for him. Everyone thought he would be the family star, though in what capacity, no one was quite sure. His parents, your grandparents, were itinerant Pentecostal preachers. They preached hellfire and brimstone, not unlike Billy Sunday from the early 1900s. Pentecostals* were also known for "speaking in tongues" and for rolling in the aisles of churches and tents during revivals, ergo the moniker Holy Rollers.

Howard did some childhood evangelizing but really hit his stride after graduating from high school. His parents, again your grandparents, were dirt poor, with nine kids, so there was no money for college. Howard tried his luck as an itinerant preacher. Working out of East Texas as his home base, he traveled to the small towns in the area— Lufkin, Nacogdoches, Jasper, Kirbyville, Woodville, even up to the big city of Tyler. There was no salary for an evangelist, so he relied on donations, or offerings, from the church and revival attendees. It was a subsistence living, but with no wife or kids, Howard could take decent care of himself.

He was a good-looking man, with black eyes and wavy black hair, and had a penchant for the ladies. Unfortunately for him, the ladies had a penchant for him as well, so he found himself in many awkward situations, especially considering he was a man of the cloth. He got in trouble in almost every town he preached in, getting caught sleeping with church deacons' wives and daughters and with parishioners. By 1955, he was broke and accused of fathering three children. He woke up one morning and hit the road, fleeing to the state of Oklahoma.

He spent the last few bucks he had on a fleabag motel for a week's stay and breakfast at a local diner outside Oklahoma City. Over coffee, he scanned the local paper for jobs and saw an advertisement for a salesman for the Fuller Brush Company. He was a natural and soon became the leading door-to-door salesman Fuller Brush ever had. He met a woman, got married, had two sons, and had some stability in his life for once.

He moved on from Fuller Brush, much to the company's dismay, and worked for Sunbeam Vacuum Cleaners for a while. That was not nearly as lucrative, so he moved on after a year and took a job with the National Bible Company. He was again a natural. He knew the Bible from spending half his life in church and from his preacher days, and he again became the leading door-to-door salesman for National.

But somewhere along the line, Howard got a taste for whiskey. Maybe it was genetic, maybe it was from all the traveling, or maybe it had something to do with religion and his failure to uphold his parents' ideals. He slowly descended into chronic drunkenness. He lost his job, his wife, still in Oklahoma City, took the kids and left him, and again he was destitute.

By 1962, he was riding the rails, or "hoboing," picking up odd jobs where he could and spending his money on bad wine. It was during this time that he probably encountered Lester Mimms in the Katy Railroad yards outside Oklahoma City. Even though Mimms was still a yardmaster, he probably had thrown Howard off a few trains. Mimms became a bull in 1966, and shortly thereafter, from what I found in the union records, Mimms became a "traveling bull."

So, it seems that Howard traveled, panhandled, and worked odd jobs while Mimms, working as a railroad policeman, acted on Howard's behalf by allowing him to travel free on the Katy Railroad. And all possibly went well until the shooting in July 1972.

From what I can gather, Howard moved back to Zavalla, Texas, after the shooting, sobered up, got back together with his wife and sons, went to a Methodist seminary, and got his preacher's license. How he afforded that, I have no clue. His record has been clean as a whistle since then, and he maintained his job as pastor of Memorial Methodist Church in Jasper for over ten years, having taken a few assistant pastor jobs along the way to hone his skills.

He and his family lived on some Peck family property in Zavalla that he had inherited, and he commuted to Jasper until he was recently debilitated by cirrhosis and liver cancer. The rest is history. I'm assuming the family still lives on the Zavalla property, but you'll be able to find that out at the funeral. Sorry I won't be able to make it.

Hope all this helps.

Love, J. J.

CHAPTER 24

THE FUNERAL

Friday, September 13, 2002

We were on the road to Jasper by 8 a.m. Around ten o'clock, I stopped at one of those all-in-one service-station facilities in the heart of the piney woods. The regular gas pumps were lined up on one side of the property, diesel facilities on the other, and inside the store was the best fried chicken on the planet. I got a sack full of chicken tenders and a fist full of paper towels, since I didn't know when I'd be eating again. I didn't want to risk the dreaded hypoglycemia.

Mary Louise got back in the truck following her potty break and looked at the sack.

"Smells good. Fried chicken?"

"Yep, tenders. Have one."

She rummaged through the sack, took out a tender, and took a tentative bite. "Yum. That's really good," she said, and put the remainder back in the sack.

"You can eat the whole thing. I bought plenty."

"A girl my age has to watch her figure."

"How about this? You eat, and I'll watch your figure."

She was decked out in a black jacket, black blouse, and black skirt that came just above her knees. The package looked like designer duds to me, but then I couldn't tell the difference between Chanel and "Flannel." She had removed her wide-brimmed black hat to get back in her seat.

"You're looking mighty spiffy today, Mrs. Brady."

"Why thank you, Dr. Brady. You're looking pretty handsome yourself. I'm used to seeing you in scrubs, but it's nice to see you in a black suit with a tie once in a while."

"When that happens, usually someone is dead."

We had left Tip at the kennel, since we were going to be on the road for a couple of days. The last time he was dropped off there, Mary Louise was in a coma, and he stayed for a month. He hadn't forgotten, even though it had been over a year, or so his facial expression seemed to say when I waved goodbye.

"I've been giving a lot of thought to the offer from the Sanders family. That would be a life-changing gift."

"Yes, it would," my bride said. "A lot of doors could open up for you. You'll just have to decide what it is you would like to do with your time. You wouldn't have to work if you didn't want to, or you could be a part-time surgeon if you wanted to keep your hand in the business."

"I don't think you can be a part-timer in my business. I might have to think about practicing a different sort of medicine. I have looked at our finances and I spoke to our investment advisor early this morning. You know that we've been trying to save money every month for years, trying not to live extravagantly, and in spite of that, my IRA has grown but not nearly enough to retire on. With this bequest of the Sanders, we could invest it in tax-free municipal bonds, live off the interest, and not have to touch the principal."

"What kind of interest rate would we get on that amount of money?"

"The money manager told me that the longer you extend out the maturities, the higher the return rate. Of course, there are fluctuations in interest rates, and sometimes the principal can look bleak if rates go up, and sometimes the principal can look stellar if rates go down. Let's say that we put the entire $16,162,448 into thirty-year munis at 6 percent. That would produce an annual tax-free revenue of close to $1,000,000, which, after management fees, would leave you and I a small fortune, tax-free, to live on.

"So, husband of mine, you could invest that money, quit working yourself to death, do what you want for the rest of your life, and make four times the money you're making now? What am I missing?"

"No idea, but it sounds pretty logical when you put it in perspective. But I sure would miss those insurance-company letters and phone calls . . ."

We had a good laugh.

We arrived in Jasper at eleven thirty and decided to see if we could check in early so we could unload the car before the funeral, burial service, and reception after.

The hotel was nothing special, but the clerk had our room ready, so we unloaded the car, freshened up, watched a little news on the TV, then headed over to the church. The parking space for our "deluxe" room was conveniently right in front of the entry door, so at least there was that luxury.

The funeral was to be at the Memorial Methodist Church, Howard's pastorate for the past ten years. It was an old-fashioned structure of red brick intermixed with siding. There was the traditional cross on the roof over the entry. The vestibule was shallow and narrow and spilled into the seating area. The sanctuary held a couple of hundred people, I guessed, with three seating sections separated by two aisles. The pulpit was elevated, behind which was a choir loft with maybe twenty voices seated, leafing through sheet music.

The usher asked if we were family of the deceased, which we affirmed, and he led us down the left side of the sanctuary. The first three rows were reserved for family, so we entered the third row and sat. I noticed Lela Belle Peck, wife of the deceased, seated in the front row, surrounded by women and men ranging from their forties to their seventies, and youngsters I assumed to be her grandchildren.

I should have known all these people, as they were my aunts and uncles and cousins, but having excused myself from family gatherings since I was a teen, I did not.

As we sat, two rows of faces in front of us turned in unison and stared for a moment. I gave a gentle nod to the crowd, as did Mary Louise. They whispered among themselves for a moment, then turned again in unison toward the pulpit. Only one little lady with silver hair kept her eyes on us, smiled, then waved at us with her fingers. I couldn't remember which one she was, since there were eight sisters, but I managed to remember all their names: Laura, Leah, Lillian, Linda, Lorene, Lucille, Lydia (who didn't like her first name and went by her middle name, Mildred, whom I had operated on), and Lyla. I returned the wave to one of the "L" sisters.

There was a commotion in the rear of the sanctuary, and as one might expect, it was my mother, Lucille. She was talking loudly to one of the ushers, then stormed off down the aisle without waiting for her escort. She arrived at our row, made a shooing gesture with her hand, and sat beside me.

"Did you look at your uncle?"

"No."

"You have to go up and view the body. It's an open casket. And you must greet the widow and her immediate family. That's only polite, and of course, customary."

"Mother, I've seen plenty of deceased people in my life, and I don't need to see another, even if he's my uncle."

She reached around me to take hold of Mary Louise's arm, pulled her, which canted me in her direction, and forced the three of us to stand. She held onto my wife with one hand, and me in the other, and led us to the casket.

"He looks good for being so sick for so long, don't you think?" she asked in our general direction. Mary Louise and I simply nodded, as my better angels encouraged my silence. Mother then abruptly turned and led us to the front row, where we were literally forced to shake hands with everyone sitting there. The "waver" stood up and gave M. L. and I a hug, after which we returned to our third-row seats. I still didn't know which sister she was, but she seemed to bear us no ill will.

The choir started a rendition of Denise Williams's song "I Come to the Garden Alone." The twenty voices sounded much larger, what with the backup band of piano, Hammond B-3 organ, bass guitar, and tenor sax. The music was very good and seemed to put the collective audience in a tearful and reflective mood. As the choir began "The Old Rugged Cross," a man dressed in a purple cassock, who I assumed to be the eulogist, entered the platform from behind the choir loft.

"Let us stand in remembrance of our beloved pastor, Howard Peck."

And that's when I turned off my conscious thinking process. I knew more about Uncle Howard than anyone in this building, I would imagine. Except for his sisters, these folks in attendance probably only knew Howard since his conversion back to reality thirty years ago, when he gave up the hobo life and the drinking, returned to his wife and children, and became a minister. I paid no attention to the service but rather thought of ways to sequester Lela, Ron, and Rico so that I might question them about their decision to sue University Medical Center and Hospital, as well as Lela's deceased husband's treating physicians.

The next thing I remember was Mary Louise getting me to stand up for the benediction. "I'm going to ride with you to the graveside service," my mother said.

I'd rather have a stick in my eye, or better yet, go to a bar, was my initial thought for a response. But again, my better angels had apparently taken over for the day, and I was silent.

We stood as Lela, Ron, Rico, and assorted "close" family members passed by the casket. Lela laid a white rose inside the coffin, wiped tears from her cheeks, turned to her sons, and made her way up the aisle and left the church.

We three joined the procession to the graveside, which, with our police escort, took only five minutes. Jasper was not a big town. Carloads of mourners made their respective ways to the burial site, where we stood at least ten deep to hear the final words of the eulogist. I didn't catch his name, but he did a fine job talking about a man whom he obviously hadn't known prior to 1972. Ron Peck, the minister, said a few generic words about his father and returned to his seat next to his mother. I heard "Ashes to ashes, dust to dust," and my wandering psyche returned to the happenings. Lela, Ron, and Rico each threw a handful of freshly dug dirt onto the coffin, and Howard Peck was laid to rest.

CHAPTER 25

THE RECEPTION

Friday, September 13, 2002

We returned to the church recreation center for socialization and refreshments. I looked for scotch or vodka at the card-table-turned-bar and found diet sodas and lemonade. I longed for a good old-fashioned Catholic wake.

While many of those present were my relatives—aunts, uncles, and cousins—I felt like a stranger in their midst. That of course was my own fault, having detached myself from the Peck family years ago. None of the Pecks lived in the West Texas area where I grew up. They were mostly an East Texas varietal family.

Several folks came up and said hello to Mary Louise and me, and although I tried to respond with pleasantry, my heart just wasn't in it. My goal was to talk to Lela, Ron, and Rico, and I sensed they were doing their dead-level-best to ignore me. Finally, Mary Louise went up to Lela when she was alone, gave her a hug, and brought her reluctantly to where I was standing.

"I need a moment of privacy with you and your sons, Lela."

"Not a good time, Jim Bob. I buried my husband today, in case you weren't paying attention."

"I've been here all day, Lela, and I was with Howard in the hospital, in case you have forgotten."

"And you and your people killed him."

"Lela, the doctors treating Howard did not kill him. He had cirrhosis of the liver, and liver cancer, and, as it turns out, pancreatic cancer to boot. He was a dead man undergoing a heroic surgery to try and save his life."

"He shouldn't have had the transplant at all. The other doctors told me he wasn't a candidate for a transplant due to the cancer. So, what little time I might have had left with him, you and your people took away."

"Lela, what other doctors are you talking about? The medical records that I reviewed read that you had taken him to the ER in Zavalla due to excoriated skin from scratching, and that once they had reviewed his lab work, they put him in an ambulance and sent him to Houston."

"I'm talking about the doctors in Tyler, at East Texas Medical Center. When he first turned yellow, I took him up there."

"When was this?"

"Three months ago, maybe four now. They did a workup, lab tests, scans, a liver biopsy, the whole shebang. We asked about the liver transplant, but they said he wasn't a candidate due to the cancer. So, I took him back home to die. The only reason I took him to Zavalla that night was to get some medication for the itching. He was scratching himself bloody. The doctor there ran some blood work, which looked like it scared him to death, and called for an ambulance. He knew someone down there in Houston he thought could help Howard. I wanted to go back to Tyler, since we'd been there and I have relatives there, but the doc in the ER said he needed to go to Houston."

Ron and Rico stepped up about that time, shook my hand, and gave Mary Louise a hug. "Sorry for your loss, boys," I said. "Your dad was an interesting fellow. I'm sure he'll be missed. I was just having a discussion with your mother about your decision to sue the hospital and the doctors that were treating him."

Ron, the preacher, spoke first. "I'm not in favor of it. I spent almost a week down there, and I have to say that the staff we dealt with were the best. The doctors, the nurses, even the kitchen folks that brought Dad his food were caring, and polite, and seemed to have Dad's best interests at heart. I understand that without the transplant, Dad had a very short expected lifespan. And who knows what kind of condition he would have been in during that time. But I went through a lawsuit once before after an auto accident, and it just about did me in. I really don't think anyone won, when it was all said and done, except the lawyers, and they always get their pound of flesh. I've discouraged Mom from proceeding."

Rico had a different take, and he was a total opposite from Ron. I had been told he was a jeweler and pawn-shop owner, but he was rough around the edges, and in my opinion, more pawn-shop owner than jeweler.

"Well, I've still got stitches in from where they took out part of my liver, and I'll never get that back. Sure, the docs told me it would regenerate in time, but right now I'm missing half my liver. I could have avoided all that if the Houston doctors had just told us what the Tyler doctors told us—no transplant due to the cancer."

Ron and Rico's respective wives came up and introduced themselves to Mary Louise and me. Ron's wife was plain and polite, Rico's loud and laden with gold jewelry.

"Thanks for your time," I said, to all parties present. "I'm sure we'll see each other before too long, if you proceed with the lawsuit. I will of course do everything in my power to aid and abet University Hospital and my colleagues."

As Mary Louise and I walked away, in search of the nearest establishment that served alcohol, my mother called out.

"Where are you two going? The party's not over yet. I want you to visit with your relatives. You haven't seen them in years."

"Mother, I've had enough mingling with my relatives to last me a long time. Are you taken care of for the night? I wouldn't want you driving back home in the dark."

"Yes, I'm staying with Lorene."

"Good. See you . . . whenever."

The Pig and Whistle was within walking distance of our hotel. We sat at the bar and ordered Tito's dirty martinis with regular olives, and chicken wings.

"Some family, huh? Sorry to put you through that."

"I married you for better or for worse, remember? I don't know what to say about Lela and her sons. I thought that Ron was a gentleman, but Rico seemed to be a catalyst for the lawsuit."

"I agree. I'll have to call Ben Silverman on Monday and get the details as to whether or not the Pecks have filed a lawsuit already. If so, that's very quick; it usually takes weeks or even months to get enough data to file a medical malpractice claim. There must be something else going on if a lawsuit has already been filed.

"And there is something else that I can't stop thinking about. Lela and Rico kept talking about the cancer, that the doctors at East Texas Medical Center wouldn't recommend a liver transplant due to the cancer. Were they talking about the liver cancer, or about the pancreatic cancer? Our people in Houston didn't know about the pancreatic cancer until it was discovered during Uncle Howard's operation. If the oncologist had known about the second cancer, he would not have recommended the transplant in the first place. Which makes me wonder if the ETMC docs had seen the pancreatic cancer on his scans, which is why they would not recommend the liver transplant. Our docs only saw the liver cancer, although the pancreatic cancer was diagnosed postmortem by the pathologist, who happened to be Jeff Clarke. But all agreed at the M&M conference that the pancreatic cancer could not be seen in any of the scans they reviewed. That is a real fly in the ointment."

We sipped our drinks for a quiet moment. "By the way, I have a favor to ask you."

"What's that, husband? You know your wish is my command. Not exactly, but you get my drift."

"I want to go see Lester Mimms. Fort Worth is about a four-hour drive. We could drive over in the morning and meet with him, see the sights and spend the night in the old Stockyards Hotel."

"I read J. J.'s file on Howard Peck this morning before we left. The interaction between him and Lester Mimms over the several years they had a relationship is very interesting. I'd like to see for myself how this all turns out, so I'm game. By the way, how would you know Mr. Mimms is available unless you've already called him?"

I winked at her.

CHAPTER 26

LESTER MIMMS

Saturday, September 14, 2002

We reached the eastern edge of the Dallas–Fort Worth Metroplex at eleven in the morning, but it took another hour through freeway crawl to reach Arlington Heights in Fort Worth. As a kid, my parents took me there a couple of times to visit Dad's sister and her husband, a paperman for the *Fort Worth Star Telegram*. Uncle Leo was a pipe smoker and used this incredibly aromatic tobacco. I can still smell it after all these years.

Arlington Heights is a bucolic neighborhood in the middle of the Fort Worth metropolis, near the Fort Worth Botanic Garden. Its boundaries are Camp Bowie to the west, University Drive to the east, and Interstate 30 to the south. We wandered a bit, looking for Lester Mimms's home, and finally found the one-story structure on a large lot with many oak and elm trees. The house appeared to be freshly painted, and the yard was well kept. The porch was deep and wrapped around the house like a gallery in south Louisiana, leaving plenty of room to sit outside and enjoy the rain without getting wet.

When I spoke to him on the phone the day before, I introduced myself as a doctor in Houston and a nephew of Howard Peck, and that I was attending his funeral in Jasper and wanted to see him on behalf of my deceased uncle. I assumed he hadn't had contact with his old traveling buddy for thirty years. He was quite pleasant on the phone and said he would be happy to meet with me.

When I rang the doorbell, the door opened immediately, followed by the outside screen. "Are you Dr. Brady?" he asked.

"Yes sir, and this is my wife, Mary Louise."

We all shook hands and he invited us in. He used a cane to ambulate and was not what I would call a large man. The Mutt moniker than Evelyn Jacoby had used no longer applied to Lester Mimms. He was about my height and weighed maybe 150 pounds. His pallor had me suspecting cancer at first glance.

"It's noon, so I assumed you folks would be hungry. I had my housekeeper make finger sandwiches. Beer, wine, or soda?" he asked.

I liked this man already. I glanced around while he was in the kitchen. The house was immaculate and well decorated in a modern style. I didn't see a single doily.

He returned with a large tray of food, including sandwiches and chips and a bottle of cold pinot grigio. "Help yourself," he said. I poured wine for the three of us and scarfed down a couple of sandwiches, which were delicious, by the way.

"Mr. Mimms, you may find it odd that I located you. It took a lot of doing."

"Well, I'm in the phone book," he laughed.

"Had I known your name, I would have called earlier."

I told him the story about the most incredible coincidence of me being the treating physician in the University General ER when he arrived July 1, 1972, about the opening of his chest and the transfer to the OR, and the repair of his pulmonary artery by Dr. Dewey Moss.

"I should have looked you up and thanked you at the time for saving my life, but I wasn't in a good place at that point in time."

"Well, sir, I should have done the looking. I didn't even follow up on your care and find out your name. It was unforgiveable, really.

That wasn't my greatest era either, I must say. I'm just glad we both survived."

With that, we toasted and ate in a comfortable silence.

"What kind of physician are you, Jim?"

"I'm an orthopedic surgeon, still working with the same institution where I trained and first met you."

"I see. And you, dear?" he asked of Mary Louise.

"I was in retail for a long time but eventually retired and stayed home to take care of my husband and our son J. J. They both seem to need a lot of care, even now."

He laughed at that, then said, "I have lung cancer. I was a smoker of those unfiltered cigarettes for too many years. I was in the army for ten years. Did you know they used to put cigarettes in our MREs?"

"Sorry. MREs?"

"Food rations. You weren't in the military?"

"No. I was drafted after medical school but classified 4-F by the examining doctor because I had rheumatic fever when I was twelve years old. I guess the army didn't want to possibly have to pay for heart trouble."

"Like flat feet and migraines."

"Yes, sir. What's the status of your lung cancer? If you don't mind me asking."

"Not at all. Initially I had a lobectomy, since the cancer was confined to one small area. When it spread, I started radiation therapy and chemotherapy. All that has failed, and I'm on my last leg now. Doc here gives me six months maybe. So, I'm tying up loose ends in my life, and that's why I wanted you to come and visit. Howard Peck was a large part of my life. You say you were at his funeral?"

"Yes, yesterday. He had severe cirrhosis of the liver and liver cancer. He had an attempted liver transplant last week but died of uncontrollable bleeding on the operating table. I saw him the day before his surgery, and he gave me a mission to find your family and make amends for the shooting. The main problem was that, to him, your name was Bull. Maybe he knew your real name, maybe he didn't, but having only Bull to go by made finding you difficult. Plus, he thought he'd killed you. At any rate, here I am, to make amends for my uncle, Howard Peck."

"How much do you know about Preacher and me? I mean, you found me without knowing my name, so you must have had some professional assistance."

"Yes. Our son has a private investigation firm. He was a great asset. In fact, why don't I give you a summary of what we know about your life and you can fill in the blanks? You were born in Edmond, Oklahoma, in 1929. After high school graduation in 1947, you joined the army and rose to the rank of Master Sergeant. Something happened in 1957—the information was redacted on the document I reviewed—and you left the service with an honorable discharge. You went to work for the Katy Railroad in Edmond, then five years later moved to Fort Worth. You've worked as a switchman, a yardmaster, and a railroad police officer. We put you as having been in contact with Howard Peck in the mid-1960s, after which you became some sort of "traveling" police officer. You and my uncle hitchhiked to Kitty's Purple Cow on July 1, 1972, where you were shot. After you recovered, you returned to work at the Katy until your retirement in 1994. What we don't know was your relationship to Howard, or what you did at the railroad after you were shot, or why you were shot to begin with."

He stared at me for a moment, then looked at Mary Louise and said, "You have a pretty smart husband and son, ma'am. I think they know more about me than I do myself."

"Well, when my husband gets a bee in his bonnet, he doesn't let go of a problem until he solves it. Our son inherited that gene."

"Excuse me for a moment, please," Mimms said, and disappeared toward the kitchen.

"What do you think, M. L.?" I whispered.

"Seems like a nice fellow. There's something else going on, though, I can feel it."

Mimms returned with fresh ice in a crystal bowl and a second bottle of pinot grigio already open.

"I find that alcohol eases the pain of the metastases in my spine. So does marijuana, but we can't talk about that."

"That comes under patient–doctor confidentiality, so not to worry—may I call you Les?"

"Of course. So let me tell you about Preacher. I ran into him the first time when I was a yardmaster here in Fort Worth, between 1962 and 1966. He was an unusual character in that he was always well-groomed and well-dressed. He wore this gray fedora hat with a feather in the band, and unless it was terribly hot, a suit jacket. He was recognizable from a distance. Some of the men that were riding the rails in those days were not so well-dressed, and rarely bathed.

"I saw him climbing into a freight car when I was at the yardmaster station, which had a wall of windows so I could see what was going on in the yard. We had police officers that worked for the Katy, but I couldn't find anyone at the time, so I left my post and went into the yard and confronted him in the railcar. He said he was desperate to get down to Waco to see an ill sister but had no money, and he hoped I would show him a little kindness. So, I let him go. I saw him a few more times after that, always clean, always dressed well. I basically just left him alone.

"In 1966, the stress of the yardmaster job finally got to me, and I applied for a bull position, railroad police. I worked the yards around Fort Worth and saw Preacher more often. He would strike up a conversation, ask me if I was ready to meet Jesus if I died today, comments and questions like that. Generally, the men that rode the rails liked him and gave him the name Preacher because he was always trying to save somebody's soul. Also, he knew the Bible backward and forward, and man, could he quote scripture. I wasn't much of a religious man at the time, so I found his abilities quite alluring.

"I don't know how it happened, actually, but gradually I became very attached to the man. I didn't get to see him very often, even being a bull, because Preacher was constantly on the go between Oklahoma City and Galveston. I was drawn to him like a moth to the flame, so I engineered a bull position that allowed me to travel on the rails while maintaining my position of authority in the various towns the Katy serviced. I was shocked when the bosses said okay to my plan.

"Once I was a traveling cop, Preacher and I were together a lot, probably too much. I gradually became totally infatuated with him and wanted to spend all my time with him. I had deep feelings for him. I told him on many occasions that I loved him. I wanted a physical relationship with him, but he resisted that. I found out he had a wife and two sons in Oklahoma City and was very guilty about leaving them behind for years while he rode the rails. I don't know what motivated him, other than maybe he was running away from something, but he never shared what it was. Sometimes he would leave me for days, occasionally a week or so, and said he was out selling Bibles to get some cash.

"He was an enigma. Preached to other travelers about God, then would get on a bender and stay smashed on cheap wine for days. This went on for several years. The end came in June of 1972. Preacher had made the decision to give up the booze and the traveling and go back to his wife and his boys. They were still in Oklahoma City, but he wanted to move them to some little town in East Texas where he had been left some land, settle down, and become a preacher full time.

"I was devastated and beside myself. I concocted a story about going to Kitty's in Surfside for a final meal. He called it our 'last supper.' I arranged to catch the Katy down to Galveston, and we hitchhiked from there. I brought my little pea shooter along, a Smith & Wesson .25 six-shooter. My plan was to shoot him right then and there, after we ate, then turn the gun on myself. As it happened, whether he suspected something or not, he was wary. I stood up at the outside table we were eating at, said something to the effect that I was sick and tired of this, and pulled the gun out. We struggled, the gun went off, I went down, and that's the last thing I remember until I woke up in the hospital in Houston a few days later."

I didn't know what to say. Mary Louise asked, "So you loved him but it was unrequited?"

"I think he loved me, but he was too hung up on the Bible, and memories of growing up in the Pentecostal church, and guilt over his family. We touched each other only on the rare occasion, after which he would leave for days."

"Did you ever marry or have children?" she asked.

"No, ma'am. I never considered myself a queer—I guess that would be gay, now—but more of a eunuch. I've had a good life, no regrets. I just managed to live without physical affection, except for a couple of old-maid sisters of mine who give me the occasional hug."

"And you never saw Howard again, or tried to get in touch with him, or he you?

"No, ma'am. After I recovered from the gunshot wound, I thought it best to let sleeping dogs lie."

"What did you do for the railroad after you recovered from the shooting?" I asked.

"I went back to the yardmaster job. That seemed a lot less stressful than following Howard around for all those years."

"I heard you call him Howard. You knew his real name, and he knew yours?"

"Oh sure. Though I suppose it's possible he forgot mine over the years, especially considering how much alcohol he'd had in his system during our days together."

"But you never tried to contact him?"

"No. We were both alive, and I felt it was best to leave it at that."

"And all this time, he thought he'd murdered you." We three just shook our heads at the mysteries of life.

I stood and stretched my back. "Thanks for your hospitality. I have a nice buzz on, thanks to you."

"I hope you're staying the night."

"Yep. We're going cowboy, staying at the Stockyard Hotel."

"Get the ribeye steak charred medium rare. Nothing better."

I thought for a minute. "Tell you what. How about we bring you down to Houston for a final assessment before we just assume you're going to die. I'm sure the doctors here in Fort Worth are excellent, but there is a lot of research going on with immunotherapy for lung cancer, and the early results have been quite favorable. We have an outstanding cancer hospital on the campus of the University Medical Center, and now that I know you, I'd like you to give my colleagues a chance to at least evaluate you. I'm not promising anything, but—"

"Yes," he said, before I could finish the sentence. "What do I have to lose?"

"I'll be in touch." He and I shook hands, and Mary Louise of course gave him one of her hugs that could cure anything that ails. I saw his eyes well up with tears as she kissed him on the cheek.

CHAPTER 27

LAWSUIT

Saturday, September 14, 2002

We went for a walk after we checked into the Stockyards Hotel, and we nearly were run over by the Fort Worth Herd, a daily Texas longhorn cattle drive through the Stockyards National Historic District. There were real cowboys and cowgirls on horses, though. Yee haw!

The desk clerk assigned us to the Bonnie and Clyde Room, which was the actual room occupied by Bonnie Parker and Clyde Barrow during their stay in Fort Worth in 1933. I practiced quick draw with Bonnie's .38 revolver. Fun!

Texas Christian University was playing at home that night, so the town was packed. Rather than drive around and fight the crowds, we opted to take Les Mimms's advice and eat at the Stockyards Hotel. I had the rib eye charred medium rare as recommended. It was delicious, but so large I felt like I was eating a whole cow. Mary Louise opted for the petite filet, a much smaller choice. There was room on her plate for other delectables such as a baked potato and fresh green beans. We ordered a bottle of Jordan Cabernet Sauvignon with dinner. All in all, it was a fine dining experience.

I watched the Horned Frogs game against Dallas rival Southern Methodist University on TV and I dozed intermittently, thinking off and on about Lester Mimms and my Uncle Howard. It was quite a story, to say the least. Had I done the right thing by inviting Les to come down to Houston and get another battery of tests? Mary Louise thought so. I tried to get her to affirm our decision, but she was beyond dozing; she was at the purring stage. It wasn't that late, but it had been a long day. I've never understood why traveling four hours in the car is so tiring. I mean, you're sitting down, not pedaling or anything, expending no calories. In my case, I gained calories with those chicken tenders, and they were probably why I was so weary, trying to metabolize all those carbs. I dropped off to sleep wondering if my belt would be tight on the four-hour morning drive back to Houston.

Dr. Ben Silverman, president and CEO of University Hospital, called me on my car phone on our trip home to confirm that my aunt and her sons had already filed a lawsuit against University Hospital, Dr. Crawford, Dr. Robert Damon the oncologist, and the radiologist who had read the scans on her deceased husband/their father, my uncle, Howard Peck. Ben said that any help on my part would be appreciated.

"You should know, Ben, that I'm on the hospital's side on this one. I had a talk with her at my uncle's funeral. The minister son was not in favor of the lawsuit, but the pawn-broker son was very aggressive about it. You should also know, and I'll be happy to discuss with the doctors involved, that the family had sought treatment elsewhere around four months prior to coming to UMC. And when Uncle Howard had the workup there, my aunt told me, the doctors did not recommend him having a liver transplant because of the cancer. As you know, my uncle had a hidden pancreatic cancer that was discovered intraoperatively, which was the cause of his demise. He basically bled to death. There was no evidence of that cancer preoperatively. The scans were reviewed by our radiologist as well as by Jeff Clarke. So, I am confused about which cancer the docs in East Texas were talking about, provided my aunt has the facts straight."

"I reviewed the chart, and there is nothing mentioned about a prior workup except the visit to the ER, in a town called Zavalla, for severe itching. I have the chart note from the ER doctor. He ran some blood tests on Mr. Peck because of his color and skin condition and was apparently shocked to see how high the bilirubin was. He called a friend here, which happened to be Dr. Damon, and initiated the transfer. What other facility did they visit?"

"She said East Texas Medical Center, in Tyler."

"I'll have our people get right on that. We'll need those records as soon as possible. I don't think I've ever been involved in medical malpractice litigation this soon after an incident. It's almost like we were baited or something."

"I'll admit, Ben, neither have I. It'll be interesting to see how this plays out."

"Safe travels. We'll visit more later."

I dropped off Mary Louise at home and went to my office to review the cases for Monday. I stopped at the vet clinic on the way and picked up Tip. He jumped, ran in circles, chased his tail, and howled, all to let me know he was pissed that he had to spend the weekend in the kennel but was now happy because I had returned and rescued him from a fate worse than death. I felt myself a dog whisperer extraordinaire, being able as I was to interpret Tip's histrionics.

Five cases were on the schedule for the following day: two virgin knee replacements, two HTOs, and Princess Sara's hip replacement. An HTO is a high tibial osteotomy, done for genu varum—also known as bowleggedness—which causes arthritis to develop in the knee joint on the inside compartment. The surgeon would take a wedge of bone out of the tibia, or shin bone, on the outside of the knee joint, close the wedge, and staple the osteotomy cut closed. This procedure would hopefully buy eight or ten years of time before a knee replacement was necessary and was usually done for younger patients in whom arthritis had not developed throughout the entire knee joint.

Since I had left for Jasper on Friday morning, my desk had reaccumulated quite a bit of paperwork debris. I signed documents, dictated a couple of op reports that I had missed, and wrote a few letters to whiny insurance-company doctors who were trying to deny surgical repairs to my patients. It was a continuing battle, dealing with the insurance-company docs on one hand and the patients on the other. The patient's question was always the same: how can an insurance company I pay premiums to deny approval for an operation that is obviously medically indicated? My answer was always the same: because they're assholes.

Score one for taking the retirement package and hitting the road, Jack. I was planning on keeping a pros-and-cons list to help with my decision-making, and Number ONE on the pro list was distancing myself from insurance-company doctors and case managers and having to ask permission to take care of my patients.

I asked Tip what he thought I should do. Good boy that he was, he put his front paws on my thighs and worked them up toward my shoulders while I sat in my office chair. He gave my face a big lick. Which meant he didn't care what I did as long as he was with me.

I completed my paperwork like the good boy I always had trouble being, and I headed home. I planned to call Dr. Robert Damon after surgery the following day and get the ball rolling on bringing Lester Mimms to Houston for his lung-cancer evaluation. I planned also to try and facilitate getting medical records on Howard Peck from East Texas Medical Center, although I was sure Ben Silverman's people could probably handle that. In my opinion, however, two squeaky wheels were better than one, so I planned to follow through, regardless of whoever else was involved.

I looked up Ben Silverman's number in the UMC directory and dialed his cell number.

"Ben, I forgot to ask when we spoke earlier, what law firm filed suit against the hospital?"

"I have the paperwork nearby. Hang on."

I heard paper shuffling, then, "John Quinlan and Associates. Do you happen to know him?"

"Oh, yes. He was my patient some years ago. He had a hip impingement problem and a torn labrum that required arthroscopic surgery, and later on, I repaired his fractured kneecap. He did well after both procedures, but don't think I wasn't scared shitless for two years until the statute of limitations ran out."

"That bad, huh?"

"John is the king of torts when it comes to breast implants and oil and gas disasters, like refinery explosions. I'm a little surprised he's taking on a potential medical malpractice lawsuit. On occasion, he's called me and asked my advice on cases brought to him for litigation. I'd didn't hear from him on this one, for obvious reasons. Maybe he has an underling on the case, since he's added 'Associates' to the firm name."

"None of this is good news. I'm going to assemble the physicians named in the lawsuit one day this week. I'd like you to be present."

"Not a problem, Ben."

CHAPTER 28

ODDS AND ENDS

Monday, September 16, 2002

The week was uneventful, thank you very much. No wound infections, no surgical disasters, no lawsuits against me, and few "justification letters for surgery" that required dictation to an insurance company. All in all, I thought I could continue practicing medicine for a while longer if there were more weeks like that one.

The lovely Princess Sara was doing quite well, participating in her therapy like a regular patient. I ran into Erik in the coffee room, a luxury item for those fortunate to be in the Abercrombie Pavilion, and he seemed none too happy.

"Doctor," he said, and nodded. "My wife is doing very well after your operation. She says she has less pain than before, so we are all grateful for that. How much longer do we stay here?"

"Well, it takes about two weeks for the skin to heal enough that I can remove the sutures. I don't see any reason to stay past that unless she has a problem doing her physical therapy, which so far, she has managed quite well."

"They are charging us $3,000 per day, American dollars."

"The Abercrombie Pavilion is a very expensive but luxurious wing of the hospital. She seems to be content here, sir."

"She is content, but I am paying the cashier daily. Can she be moved elsewhere, to a less costly room?"

"Of course. Just let me know when she wants to move, and I'll write the order."

He paused a moment. "It is unlikely that Sara will want to move, Doctor, so I was hoping perhaps you could order it done?"

"Erik, there is no medical reason to move her, so I can't order it done without her consent. Sorry."

And I knew good and well Sara would stay in her suite until discharge, unless the price of eastern European oil plummeted.

"Good day, Doctor," Erik mumbled as I left.

I spoke to a nurse in the office of Dr. Robert Damon, the oncologist, and unfortunately she told me he was at a medical convention until Thursday. I discussed the Lester Mimms case with her and she assured me she would make arrangements to have him admitted on Sunday and begin the testing process to see if he might be a candidate for immunotherapy. She seemed very efficient and knowledgeable.

I spoke to Les on the phone, told him the plan, and gave him Dr. Damon's office number in case he missed the nurse's call. He was anxious to come to Houston to do whatever would be necessary to extend his life. He sounded upbeat.

There was one small snafu, and that was that one of my fellow Tim Stacy's kids fell out of a treehouse in the back yard and broke his right femur, or thigh bone. Fortunately, our top pediatric orthopedic surgeon, Joe Frank Bennett, was around and was able to get the child into surgery within a couple of hours. He made an incision on each side of the knee and threaded two flexible titanium rods up into the femur. The beauty of that treatment was that no casting was required, only a knee immobilizer, but no weight was allowed for six weeks. Tim of course missed a couple of his shifts in the operating room, so Shelley and I had to work a little harder, and a little longer, but the cases turned out well. Besides, I had a backup plan, and if the mood struck me, I could just walk away. I was financially solvent for the first time in my life, if I took O'Leary's offer, and it was a great feeling.

Dr. Shelley Compton was turning out to be an excellent surgeon. While I was the "captain of the ship" in our academic surgical teaching program, the residents and fellows participated in surgical procedures. They used the drills, reamers, hammers, and saws; they inserted screws and plates; and they mixed cement for implants—all the procedures that comprised a day's work in the operating room.

As a surgeon, you quickly got a feel for someone that was going to able to work with their hands and not make a mess of things. I'm not the only teaching surgeon who has recommended a resident find a place in dermatology, radiology, or pediatrics because it would be best for them to redirect a career before it's too late. I was not in the business of training lousy surgeons and didn't hesitate to tell a young doctor that they had NO business in orthopedic surgery, when the occasion arose.

That said, I was thinking that perhaps Shelley might find a niche in my field of hip and knee reconstruction. She seemed to enjoy it and was good at it. I decided I would broach that subject at a later date, but I was pleased with her performance. Perhaps she could replace me?

After clinic on Thursday, Fran told me I had to attend a meeting Friday morning with Dr. Silverman and several other doctors. I was to be at the president's office at eight thirty in the morning. I of course knew this was about my aunt's lawsuit against the hospital and Howard's treating physicians. I was anxious to review the medical records from the hospital in Tyler, and I hoped Ben had all the information we needed.

Mary Louise was hungry for seafood, so we opted for Tony Mandola's Gulf Coast Kitchen. We started with ice-cold dirty martinis with regular olives, not bleu-cheese filled. We shared shrimp cocktail and oysters on the half shell, then moved to entrées. I chose Texas Red Fish Pontchartrain, and she Rainbow Trout Almondine.

We washed all that down with a bottle of pinot grigio and vanilla ice cream with chocolate sprinkles.

Back at home and in bed for the night, I told her about my pro-and-con list.

"Smart. Maybe if you write down what you're feeling, you can make an informed decision."

"I meant to ask, is there a time frame in which I have to decide whether to take the Sanders offer or not?"

"I'll review the paperwork, but I believe it's thirty days."

"Not much time, M. L."

"Jim Bob, you don't have to decide what to do with your life in thirty days, just whether or not you're going to accept their terms and take the payout, or contest the numbers and hire your own accountant and lawyer to review the proposal."

"Okay."

"What's your schedule for tomorrow, Jim Bob?"

"Rounds early, then a meeting at eight thirty in Ben Silverman's office with the doctors being sued by Aunt Lela Belle."

"Why you? You're not party to the litigation, are you?"

"No, but Ben requested my presence. Besides, I'm very interested in the case and on what basis the hospital and doctors are being sued. I forgot to ask if we're going to Galveston this weekend?"

"No, WE have a black-tie event Saturday, the annual Crohn's and Colitis fundraiser, of which I'm co-chair. Did you forget?"

"No, I never knew about it, I don't think. But no problem, because I'm sure you reminded me."

"Would you like to top off this evening by sleeping with a chairperson?"

"I would be delighted, provided you are the chairperson about which we are speaking."

"That would be me."

"Is there something special about sleeping with a chairperson?"

"Turn out that light and you'll find out."

CHAPTER 29

CONFERENCE

Friday, September 20, 2002

The president/CEOs' lavish conference room was located outside his suite of offices. I thought for a moment that I should reconsider administrative medicine and add it to my pro/con list. But that responsibility involved herding too many "cats," so I dismissed the notion in short order.

The dark mahogany table took up the center of the room, surrounded by twelve comfortable chairs covered in a burgundy fabric. The carpet was a dark gray and matched the wall coverings. There was a sideboard table with coffee, soft drinks, and ice. I suspected that if this meeting were in the late afternoon, that table would be covered in whiskey bottles.

Ben Silverman sat at one end. I took a chair next to him. Chief oncologist Bob Damon arrived and took a chair. Then a man I did not know entered the room, looking very sheepish and scared to death. I thought he must be the radiologist that read Uncle Howard's films. He nodded at me, and I stood and greeted him.

"I'm Jim Brady."

"Joe Spears."

We were waiting for Ed Crawford when the door burst open and in walked Jeff Clarke, my old friend and now deputy chief of pathology. I knew he had reviewed the scans on my uncle because he did the autopsy, so he must have something to contribute.

Once Jeff was seated, Ben spoke. "We may as well begin. Dr. Crawford is involved in an emergency dissecting aneurysm and will be late. I think you all are acquainted except perhaps for Dr. Spears, who is a new addition to the staff. How long have you been here, Joe?"

"Almost a year, sir."

"Very good. I received the medical records from East Texas Medical Center via FedEx and spent most of the day reviewing those records and doing some research on the issues involved in this case. I've made a copy for each of you and provided paper and pens in case you want to take notes.

"Let me summarize the records. Jim, Howard Peck, your uncle, had waning health for the past year or so. He had been looked after by his local MD, Dr. McClure in Jasper, who had diagnosed the cirrhosis of the liver. I do not have his records as of yet, but that material is in transit. As Mr. Peck's condition worsened, Dr. McClure referred him to East Texas Med Center six months ago for a workup. The usual tests were performed there—CT scan, MRI scan, PET scan, blood work. I have reviewed those tests as well as the notes of the physicians there, and it's clear to me that the patient in fact did have pancreatic cancer."

This started the usual physician murmuring when discussing a complex and mystifying case.

"Before I hear your input, let me finish. The tests confirmed cirrhosis, but did not—I repeat, did NOT—show liver cancer. As you all know, he was diagnosed here at UMC with cirrhosis and liver cancer, but not pancreatic cancer. The pancreatic cancer was found posthumously by Dr. Clarke at autopsy, although we now know that the massive hemorrhaging Dr. Crawford experienced during the liver transplant most certainly came from the undiagnosed, at least by us, pancreatic cancer.

"So, gentleman, it is clear to me that we at University Hospital are in fact liable for this disaster. I realize that Mr. Peck's case was presented at M&M conference, and the presenter clearly stated that in reviewing the films and scans there was no preoperative evidence of pancreatic cancer. However, we now have evidence, specifically on the PET scan done at East Texas Med, that Mr. Peck did in fact have pancreatic cancer.

"As you all well know, we wouldn't have performed a liver transplant on a man with pancreatic cancer. Liver transplants are allowed in a diseased liver only if there is no evidence of a tumor or cancer outside the liver. You also know that the decision was made in this case to transplant even with the hepatoma—the liver cancer—present, because all our studies clearly showed no evidence of cancer outside the liver.

"But sad to say, gents, we were wrong, and our collective thumbs are in the screws, so to speak. I will now welcome comments and questions."

Dr. Damon spoke first. "Ben, I've been an oncologist for over twenty years, and while I may have made a mistake along the way, I've never made a decision that cost a patient's life. I take primary responsibility for this tragedy. I've been over the scans with a microscope, and I cannot see any evidence of a pancreatic lesion on our films. I would like to compare them to the scans from East Texas Med."

"That's why I invited Dr. Jeff Clarke to this meeting. He performed the autopsy on Mr. Peck and has reviewed our scans and the scans from East Texas and will discuss his findings. Jeff?"

X-ray view boxes lined two walls in the conference room, so Jeff stood and quietly began filling the boxes with scans. When he was done, he invited us all to stand and review the films with him.

"East Texas Med did their studies six months ago. During that time, we would assume that the patient's cirrhosis worsened, and that the liver cancer predictably became larger. This type of activity would create a significant disturbance in the abdomen and would cause organ displacement and possibly a distortion in the anatomy. This could explain why our scans showed cirrhosis and liver cancer but not the pancreatic cancer.

"However, doing further research, I found that the pancreatic cancer diagnosed at East Texas Med was seen only on the PET scan. It was not picked up on either CT or MRI scan. In researching the various forms of pancreatic cancer, there are those types of adeno-carcinomas that can hide in the head of the pancreas and grow until the tumor blocks the bile duct. You've all seen patients who come in with jaundice, and think they have hepatitis, and discover they've had a cancer growing in the abdomen for a year or two.

"So, even if we have a defense against the malpractice suit that the cancer was hiding in plain sight, so to speak, and was hidden by enlargement and distortion of the liver, we cannot discount the fact that if the cancer was visible on PET scan at East Texas six months ago, we most certainly should have seen it on our scans. Our PET scan clearly did not show a pancreatic lesion, nor any lesion outside the abdomen that could be construed as a metastasis. That is confirmed by the East Texas scans. There were no hot lesions indicative of metastases seen there either, but a lesion only in the pancreas. And that is where we differ.

"And then I started thinking about isotopes. You know that the PET scan utilizes a radioactive drug as a tracer. It can be swallowed, inhaled, or injected. A lesion in the body lights up as a bright spot. And that is what was seen on the East Texas scans, a bright spot in the depths of the head of the pancreas, back behind the liver. But our scan didn't show that.

"And then I started thinking about the half-life of isotopes, or tracer drugs, and did some research. Isotopes are metabolized fairly quickly through the kidneys, as it turns out, and the literature tells us that almost 80 percent of the tracer is gone within two hours. So, the PET scan has to be performed reasonably quickly after the drug is administered, otherwise the tracer has been metabolized and the test is worthless. At East Texas Med, the scan was done within thirty minutes of injection, as is noted in the records. Dr. Spears, do you have that data for our radiology department?"

"Yes," the young doctor replied, clearly uncomfortable.

"And what say you, Doctor?" Jeff asked.

"Over two hours, actually two hours and fifteen minutes, between administration of the isotope and the scan."

There was a collective groan among the physicians in the room.

"And the reason for the delay?"

"We had an emergency that day, according to the radiology log. A patient came down for an upper GI series and started to hemorrhage after the tech gave him the barium to swallow. He lost a lot of blood quickly, and we called in a code blue. The place was in total chaos."

"And you forgot about the PET scan?"

"The staff didn't forget, they just became distracted from the code blue, and it was delayed inadvertently. The tech who was scheduled to perform the scan was said to be covered in blood and had to go shower and change, so the supervisor rotated techs."

"Did you know about the half-life of PET-scan tracer drugs and that timing of the study is critical?" Jeff asked.

"Of course. Like I said, it wasn't really radiology's fault, it was circumstances beyond my peoples' control."

"What were you doing during all this chaos, Joe?" asked Ben.

"I was in the X-ray reading room, going over films and dictating reports. You know there are rules about having a radiologic report in the medical record within twenty-four hours of a test being performed, and considering we have thousands of X-rays and scans done every day, most of the radiology docs' time is spent reviewing films and dictating our findings. That's why we have so many X-ray techs working here. Other than cardiovascular and neurological procedures, the techs do the bulk of the work."

"Well, Dr. Spears," said Ben, "this mistake cost a man his life, and that in turn is going to cost the hospital and you doctors millions of dollars. I wonder, have you had a conversation with the techs who were involved with the GI bleeder, or the PET-scan tech, to get their take on the situation, such that our liability might be mitigated?"

Poor Joe hung his head. "I have spoken to a number of techs, which is how I happen to have the information I've given you. Unfortunately, the tech originally scheduled to inject the tracer drug and perform the PET scan did not return to work after she allegedly cleaned herself up. Her name is Theresa Banfield. The supervisor hasn't heard from her, and the techs present that day told me she was new, and most were not acquainted with her."

"Who does the hiring and firing down there?" I asked.

"The radiology supervisor, who is a non-MD. The docs don't have time for that."

"So you're saying, Joe, that this tech has literally disappeared?"

Those of us at the table looked around at each other with raised eyebrows.

"That sounds suspicious to me," Ben said. "We need to check this woman out. ASAP. Meanwhile, Joe, I'm putting you on administrative leave until this situation is resolved."

"I have one question, Joe," I said. "I'm not familiar with the testing process, but why didn't you simply get another batch of isotope instead of trying to complete the PET scan with a product that was probably expired?"

"Paperwork and cost. This was a Medicare patient in an HMO as a secondary payer, and you can't just get another batch of isotope. Every aspect of a patient's care requires preapproval or nothing gets paid for—not the hospital bill, not the surgeon's bill, nothing. The supervisor made the call."

"I have one more question. If we had seen the medical records from East Texas Med, we would have been aware of the positive PET scan indicating the pancreatic tumor. And then you, Dr. Damon, would have most certainly not recommended the transplant. I don't remember, however, anyone mentioning Howard Peck's tests and treatment at East Texas Medical until his demise. Is this correct?"

"Yes," said Dr. Damon. "The family offered information about the man's treatment for severe itching at the clinic in Zavalla, after which he was referred here on an emergency basis due to his high levels of bilirubin. No one said anything about the tests at East Texas until after Mr. Peck's death, and I think it was Dr. Brady who gleaned that information from the deceased's wife."

"I think that is correct," I said. "My aunt mentioned it at the funeral, when I had a discussion with her and her two sons about the lawsuit they were planning to file. She kept saying the docs at East Texas did not recommend the liver transplant because of the cancer. I thought she was talking about the cancer IN the liver, but it turns out she was probably talking about the cancer in the pancreas, which we did not know about because our PET scan didn't show it, and because we didn't know my Uncle Howard had been through testing at East Texas and therefore we had no records to review from that institution. It seems there are mitigating circumstances in this case."

Ben said, "I don't think I've been in this situation before, gentlemen. I need to give it some thought, review the medical records from Dr. McClure in Jasper, and discuss with our legal counsel, now that I have more information. So, if there is nothing else, this meeting is adjourned."

CHAPTER 30

MR. COMPTON

Friday, September 20, 2002

Mary Louise and I decided to have lunch at Ninfa's. We love Mexican food, and I needed a serious margarita after the morning's meeting.

"Can you explain something to me, Jim? Why didn't Howard opt for any treatment when he was in Tyler? Couldn't the doctors there have done something for him?"

"I noted in the medical records that they set up an appointment for him to receive radiotherapy and chemotherapy for his pancreatic cancer, but he never showed up for treatment. We didn't really get into a discussion about that at the meeting, because that wasn't our focus. However, one of the oncologists in Tyler made a notation in the chart that the pancreatic lesion was adjacent to the superior mesenteric artery, which supplies most all the blood to the abdominal organs, which rendered the pancreatic cancer inoperable. The only treatment options available were radiotherapy and chemotherapy. I wonder, however, with him having cirrhosis of the liver, if that was even an option. I think many of those drugs are metabolized through the liver, which in Howard's case was minimally functional."

"As a lay person, I can't fathom not opting for some form of treatment, even if the odds of improvement were low."

"Mary Louise, that's one of those unanswerable questions. Howard's obviously in no condition to tell us, being dead and all, and I've found Aunt Lela to be the silent type. We'll never know, I guess. Although one thing that sticks in my craw is that while at UMC, he saw many doctors, who had many discussions about his condition, but not once did anyone mention anything about his pancreatic cancer, because we didn't know he had it. You would think he or his wife would mention to someone, 'Hey, what about the cancer in the pancreas?'"

"That artery you mentioned, was that the cause of his bleed during the attempted liver transplant?"

"Probably, although even Jeff Clarke has tiptoed around that discussion, since that could possibly imply surgeon error and further add to the hospital's liability. The party line is that during the excision of the diseased liver, or the attempted reattachment of the donor liver, or simply due to the manipulation of the internal organs during the operation, the arteries were disturbed and came loose from their moorings, and the pancreas blood supply blew like a hose."

"I don't know much about medicine except what I've learned from you over the years, but it's sad to see that Howard made a bad choice in being silent about his previous diagnosis. I know he had not one, not two, but three fatal diseases going on, but perhaps his life could have been extended for a while. I would be the kind of person to take any chance at survival. Wouldn't you, Jim?"

I would have to think about that.

Mary Louise left directly from Ninfa's and went to another board member's home to help with the decorations for the Friday-night event. We had a donor party to attend, essentially a thank you to the donors that had contributed to the CCFA and who were sponsoring the Saturday-night event. I thought I would use M. L.'s decorating time to research lung cancer and immunotherapy. I don't know why I had become involved in these two cases with cancer, except through extraordinary circumstances. I went into orthopedic surgery so I could fix things, because my personality was not designed to take care of the sick and dying. And my Uncle Howard was responsible for my involvement in his treatment, and now Les Mimms's treatment. He wanted to make amends and had selected me to carry out his wishes in some way; exactly how, was yet to be determined.

I fed Tip and took him to the doggy park for some good-natured frolicking. I figured it would do us both some good.

Upon our return, the carbohydrate loading and the margarita won out over reading and research. I laid down on the living room couch to read, and the next thing I knew, my pager was going off and I felt drool on the pillow.

"Brady."

"Dr. Brady, I'm so sorry to bother you. This is Shelley, your resident. My dad fell at the farm, and it sounds like his hip is fractured. Mom called 911, and the ambulance is on the way to the ER. Can you please come in and take a look and see what we have to do?"

"Are you there already?"

"No, sir, but I'm on my way."

"Okay, I'll be on my way in fifteen minutes."

I met Shelley's family in the ER. Mr. Compton was writhing in pain on a stretcher. His X-rays showed a subtrochanteric hip fracture with some medial wall comminution. It would require a hip screw and a side plate with compression screws. All considered, the fracture was fixable and probably with no damage to the hip joint itself.

"I've told him a million times to stay off that damn tractor. He thinks he's John Deere himself," Mrs. Compton said to Shelley and me.

"Mom, how did it happen exactly?"

"He had climbed up there just to prove he could, and he wanted to go plow up some mess down by the pond. He apparently got off the tractor down there, got his boots all wet but somehow got back on. When he reached the barn and tried to get off again, he caught his foot and fell off. He's a damn fool, your father."

"We'll be able to fix the hip, Mrs. Compton, not to worry," I said. "Do you happen to know when he ate last?"

"About an hour before he went off on the tractor. We had country fried steak and potatoes. Is that a problem?"

I looked at Shelley, and she told her mom, "Dad has to be without solid food for at least eight hours before anesthesia can put him under, and it's already 3 p.m. I think it's best to wait until first thing in the morning. Also, we'll need his cardiologist to see him. He has an arrythmia problem and takes meds for that."

"I would agree, Mrs. Compton. I'll call the OR to get a start time for the morning. Maybe you can get in touch with the cardiologist, Shelley?"

"Will do. Thanks so much for coming in."

"No problem. Nice meeting you, Mrs. Compton."

"Oh, silly, call me Liz. Everybody does."

Shelley pulled me aside. "They want to go up to Abercrombie. They always stay there."

"No problem. The hospital can always use the extra cash."

CHAPTER 31

DONOR DINNER

Friday, September 20, 2002

As I made the drive back home, I thought about Shelley's mother. Obviously well off enough to stay in the exclusive Abercrombie Pavilion—maybe her husband would end up next door to Princess Sara—she was not a typical Houston socialite. I noticed that her hands were calloused and without nail polish. She had on denim jeans, a white shirt, a denim jacket, red Roper boots, and a green felt Western hat. Her face was lined and appeared not to have had the benefit of sculpting by one of Houston's many plastic surgeons.

I had tried to introduce myself to Mr. Compton, but he was in pain due to the fracture and was in no mood to have a conversation. He was, however, happy to get a shot of morphine in his IV line.

Once home, I was immediately set upon by both Tip and Mary Louise. "Where were you? You didn't leave me a note. I called a couple of times, but the call went straight to voice mail."

"I had to make a trip to the hospital. Shelley Compton's father got his leg tangled up with a tractor while at his farm and fractured his hip. I thought I might have to fix it tonight, but he had a late lunch of steak and potatoes, so we delayed the surgery until the morning. I'm so glad I don't have to miss the donor dinner. I'm so looking forward to it," I said, with my best fake smile.

Mary Louise gave me "the look." "I detect some smartass talk there, young man. You know these charities I raise money for are near and dear to my heart."

"I know, sorry. Just a little pregame levity on my part."

"I understand your dislike for events where you have to sit between donors that you probably don't know, but sometimes they can be great fun, with the right attitude. Now I'd appreciate it if you would shower and get dressed. We have to be there early."

We arrived at a mansion just off River Oaks Boulevard at 6 p.m. River Oaks was the most exclusive neighborhood in Houston. Just ten minutes from downtown and the University Medical Center, the location was ideal for executives, attorneys, and previously, doctors, until the insurance companies invented "managed care" and decimated our fees. This home was a three-story behemoth, with a long circular driveway that extended about a quarter of a mile out to the street. It had white stucco on the exterior, with a red tiled roof and a beautiful porte cochere. A valet parker in a white dinner jacket opened Mary Louise's door, and as usual I was left to fend for myself. I brought the truck just to show that I was real a Texan and not a fake one driving a Bentley or Ferrari.

The foyer was open all the way up to the top floor, which had a dramatic effect upon entry. I'm certain it had a dramatic effect on the light bill every month, but if you could afford a house like this, who would care about utility costs? A waiter passed by with a tray full of drinks, and I grabbed one, not caring what it was, only that it contained alcohol. The event signified a long night.

After an hour or so, guests began arriving. I stood off to the side of the entry, in hopes that someone I knew and liked would be attending. And after fifteen or so minutes, and another of whatever potion the waiter was serving, Greg Mayfield walked in. Greg and I had been in medical school at the same time, trained together in orthopedics, and were partners in the UMC Orthopedic Group.

"Dude, I can't believe you're at this function."

"Since your wife Mary Louise is the chair of the event tomorrow night, Susan wouldn't let me out of it. I had to pay $1,000 a seat to eat bad food and suffer through weak drinks. I should make you reimburse me."

"You got off light, son. Hello, Susan," I said, as I leaned down and pecked her on the cheek. "Glad you two came."

"We wouldn't miss it, would we Greg?"

"Yes, dear—or is it no, dear?"

"I'm going to find some decent people to talk to," Susan said. "You two will get overserved and become obnoxious as usual. Look for your name plate, Greg. And don't switch them around like you did at the Zoo Ball."

I looked at my friend closely. "Did you really switch your name plate around? I've never had the nerve to do that."

"I always try and do it, then Susan sneaks around behind me and moves them to their original location. Let's get us a real drink, and then you can tell me about the meeting with Silverman this morning."

We found a bar toward the rear of the house, past all the tables set up in the foyer, living room, and library. As we stood and waited for our twelve-year Macallan scotches, I noticed the backyard was lit with hundreds of candles, including a number of them floating in the pool on what looked like lily pads. Folks outside were migrating back inside, it being a cool fall evening. Greg and I decided to go hide in the backyard, found a couple of lounge chairs, and sat down.

"Tell me all about it."

I gave him the rundown on the meeting that morning. I told him that Ed Crawford had not shown up, but when he heard he was going to have to pony up some money for the lawsuit, he would be breaking Silverman's door down.

"What's it going to be? Amount wise. Any idea?"

"Probably the limits per occurrence, $1 million per doctor. I don't know what the hospital will kick in. I'd love to be at that board meeting."

"I heard Quinlan had filed the suit. He won't go away cheap."

"True that. But the lawsuit was filed by Quinlan AND ASSOCIATES. That's a new moniker, and we don't have a clue if the associate is handling the case or it's Quinlan's baby. Also, there's a mystery X-ray tech that is missing from the job. Seems she disappeared about the time she was supposed to inject the isotope for the PET scan. They had a GI bleeder in radiology at the time, things got crazy, and she allegedly went to wash the blood off her hands and change clothes after the resuscitation and she never returned. Joe Spears got another tech to inject, but admitted it was late, and the PET scan didn't show my uncle's pancreatic cancer because of the short isotope half-life."

"Does that mitigate the hospital's liability?"

"No idea yet. Silverman has to find this Theresa Banfield first."

About the time the scotch was kicking in, and mellowing us out, Mary Louise found us.

"I see two partners in crime."

Greg stood and bussed her on the cheek. "You're looking fab, M. L. Let me know when you're ready to leave this loser, and we'll run away to a beach somewhere."

Mary Louise did look gorgeous, with a red dress cut low at the top, with the hem just above her ankles. Her blond hair was up, exposing that beautiful neck, with a solitary diamond pendant.

"I don't like hurricanes, Greg, and what would you propose to do about the lovely Susan, your wife?"

"I'll figure that out later."

She shook her head. "Come along boys, let's find your name plates. We're about to sit for dinner."

She stood between us, and we each took and arm and marched off in search of our terrible seating arrangements. To my great surprise, my bride had been in charge of seating, and while she did place me between a man and a woman whom I didn't know, she placed Greg directly across from me.

"I did you two boys a big favor seating you near each other. Don't make me regret it."

We were on our best behavior, although we talked about work, medical politics, football, and had a grand time. And yes, I gave both my dinner partners my attention from time to time, so as not to be rude, especially when I saw Mary Louise walking my way to assess my behavior. I didn't overserve myself, knowing I had Mr. Compton's hip to do in the morning, so what a good boy was I.

When we finally got home it was close to midnight, and Tip was ready for a trip outside. Once back safely in the apartment, I changed clothes, brushed and gargled, and put on my best Baylor University underwear and a tee shirt. I propped myself up in bed, waiting to be rewarded for being an absolutely wonderful dinner partner to the donors.

"What's that little pup tent doing in the bed with you, Jim Bob?" she asked as she exited the bathroom.

"That's no pup tent, that's a German Shepherd tent, or a Malamute tent."

"I see. I guess you're looking for a reward for your pristine behavior tonight?"

"Well, sure. Gotta throw the dog a bone when he's been good, right?"

"You're too much," she said, as she turned out the light, crawled into bed, and slung one of her long, beautiful legs over my tent.

"Ruff," I said.

CHAPTER 32

GALA

Saturday, September 21, 2002

I had booked Mr. Compton's surgery for 9 a.m. It was a nice bonus that Saturday mornings were a little more civilized than weekdays. I met Shelley in the admitting ward, we identified her father, and he was swept off to the OR. We had some coffee and a bite to eat. Normally I would let the resident perform most of the operation, which, after all, is not that hard. You open up the thigh, identify the fracture, drill a pin up into the femoral head, screw in a locking screw, wrestle—I mean manipulate—the femur bone into alignment with the femoral head, attach the side plate, apply bone clamps to hold the pieces in place, and screw in the compression screws. Mr. Compton was a fairly thin man, making the procedure easier than having to cut through a huge layer of adipose tissue (fat, to be less genteel) and clamp a lot of bleeders.

So I did the procedure, saving Shelley the angst of operating on her own father, but allowed her to close the wound while I dictated the operative report. We talked to Liz, her mother, and let her know all was well. The cardiologist would be in charge of monitoring his cardiac status and would be on the lookout for dreaded and often fatal complications such as blood clots in the legs and traveling blood clots to the lungs, called pulmonary embolisms.

"I just don't know how I'm going to handle him at home. We have a large two-story home with bedrooms upstairs."

"We can keep him here a week, maybe more, then he should go to a rehab facility so he can learn to get around. That would involve two to four weeks. By then, you'll have figured out where best to put him in the house, and it will have allowed you time to hire some nurses or nurses' aides to help you care for him," I responded.

"Thank you so much, Doctor. You're just as nice as Shelley said." Liz stood on her tiptoes and gave me a hug.

Shelley did the same, and I exited the waiting room before we all started singing "Kumbaya."

I watched college football and saw my Baylor Bears get slaughtered by Texas A&M. We would be lucky to win three games that season.

Mary Louise spent the day getting spruced up—hair, makeup, mani pedi, the works. She returned with every hair in place, little paper sandals so as not to muss the fresh toenail polish, and Kleenex around her neck so as not to stain her dress with the fresh makeup.

"Don't touch me, don't even look at me hard," was her greeting.

"I love you too," I said, sarcastically.

"We have to be there at six."

"Okay, I'll be ready. The monkey suit is all laid out."

The event was at the Ritz-Carlton, which had an enormous ballroom and plenty of room for 500 people and a large band called Sha Na Na, who specialized in song-and-dance routines to 1950s hit songs. I really enjoyed their music and the antics of lead singer Jon Bauman.

Mary Louise was decked out in a black ball gown, with diamonds on her ears, neck, and both wrists. She had on black satin high heels, which would be removed as soon as the band cranked up. I've learned, going to all these charity balls over the years, that shoes are designed for entry and cocktails only. When the music starts, the shoes come off. I would be responsible for knowing where they were at all times, however, in case shoes had to tugged on again, like, for example, going to the ladies' room.

As co-chair of the CCFA Ball, it was M. L.'s job to meet and greet and thank donors and ticket buyers for coming. I was in charge of holding up the bar and finding other stranded husbands to talk to, without becoming overserved and unable to converse with the strange people I would find at my table.

Unfortunately, I felt a tap on my shoulder, turned, and saw John Quinlan behind me.

"Evening, John."

John Quinlan was around six foot three inches tall, with brown curly hair framing an always-smiling face, partially covered by large wire-rimmed glasses.

"Evening, Brady. How are you holding up?"

"Great, thanks. Just ordered my first scotch," though unfortunately there was no Macallan at charity events because it was too expensive and the money raised was for patient care and research, not for old single-malt scotch guzzlers.

"Let me get a drink, and I'd like to visit with you away from the crowd."

I followed him to a cubbyhole off to the side of the ballroom.

"I'm sure you know I've sued UMC and four doctors for the inexcusable negligence with respect to Howard Peck. I understand he was your uncle?"

"Yes, my mother's younger brother."

"I had a conversation with Ben Silverman this morning. Seems he's willing to consider a settlement offer."

"I hadn't heard that. I can tell you that he asked me to attend the meeting yesterday morning." I didn't think it was my place to discuss the facts of the case. Eventually, smart as he was, he would figure out what we knew, and maybe he already did, but holding facts close to the vest that were not in evidence yet was the better point of valor, in my opinion.

"We're going to have a settlement conference next week. I'd like you to be there. And before you ask why, the reason is that this patient was your uncle, and cooler heads need to prevail in this situation. Your only dog in the hunt is the fact that the deceased was a relative. You're not being sued, so I would trust you to be more objective than the rest of your colleagues. This travesty is going to cost some money. We can do it the easy way, or the hard way. We can settle this out of court, and keep the reputations of the doctors, and the hospital, intact and out of public scrutiny. That is my preference. I don't want to put a grieving widow through any more emotional trauma.

"You and I have been friends for a long time. I even chose you to operate on me twice, so I trust you, which is more than I can say about most physicians. I think you're honest, and reasonable, and capable of helping settle this mess quickly and quietly. It would be in the best interests of all parties concerned." And with that said, he shook my hand, wished me a good evening, and walked away.

I think that answered our question as to who was in charge of the case, John or an "associate." Knowing him, there probably was no associate, just a word game to imply strength in numbers.

Sha Na Na was beyond great. We all danced the night away in our tuxedos, though most of the jackets, vests, and ties were gone after the second song. I did my job well, guarding the black satin pumps for their owner until it was time to go home.

CHAPTER 33

SUNDAY

Sunday, September 22, 2002

We slept in Sunday morning, exhausted from parties Friday and Saturday and the events of the past two weeks. We were starving, and nothing in the apartment seemed appropriate to alleviate our midrange hangovers. So, we dressed quickly and headed to brunch at Brennan's, a New Orleans-style restaurant with wonderful crepes, eggs Benedict, shrimp remoulade, and wood-grilled oysters. We each had to have a beverage, so we saw no reason not to wash all that tasty food down with mimosas.

That display of gluttony prompted an immediate return to bed when we arrived home, and which resulted in a two-hour nap. I probably could have slept all day, were it not for the ringing of the phone around 2 p.m.

"Dr. Brady, I'm sorry to disturb you, but you wanted to know when Lester Mimms was admitted to the hospital? Are you his treating physician?"

It took me a minute to get my bearings. "No, he's a personal friend. He should be admitted under Dr. Robert Damon, the oncology chief."

"Got it, Doctor. He'll be on the eighth floor of the oncology wing. Good afternoon, sir."

I felt the need to go see Les, and Mary Louise agreed. We showered—singularly, to my dismay—and dressed. I made a pot of orange-flavored coffee and we sipped that for a bit, then we headed over to UMC, somewhat refreshed and humanoid.

Les was in good spirits, optimistic about his chances for a prolonged survival through the magic of immunotherapy. I was lacking in information on the subject, so when he asked me what the plan was, I deferred to Dr. Damon. I had intended to brush up on the subject yesterday or today, but football, parties, eggs Benedict, mimosas, and napping had interfered. I promised myself to do some research that evening.

Mary Louise gave Les a hug, and that seemed to make his day. It occurred to me that Les had not experienced much affection in his life, and what a shame that was. He was a gentle soul, and sensitive, yet a former military man and railroad trainman. We all have different facets of our personalities, many of which are conflicting. I was no psychologist or shrink, but I had made it a habit of studying people over the years. I thought that Les Mimms was a good man, and maybe he had been dealt a bad hand of cards. Perhaps the doctors at UMC could change that. I hoped so.

We went by a specialty grocery and picked up delectables for dinner—fresh Italian bread, prosciutto, salami, black forest ham, iceberg lettuce, hothouse tomatoes, mayo and hot mustard. Mary Louise opted for another nap until dinner, while I opted to try and decipher what I could about immunotherapy for lung cancer.

Lung cancer is classified in stages. In stage 1, the cancer is limited to the lung. In stage 2, the cancer has metastasized into the local lymph nodes. In stage 3, the cancer has invaded the lymph nodes in the middle of the chest. In stage 4, the cancer has spread to other parts of the body. The survival rate for stage-4 cancer is less than one year. When we met in Fort Worth, Les said the doctors gave him six months or less to live, so that would be stage 4. That was not good.

There were several different types of lung cancer, the most common being non-small-cell cancer. Immunotherapy was indicated for this type of cancer after the first treatment modality had stopped working. In Les's case, he had a lobectomy first, followed by radiotherapy and chemotherapy. I didn't know if he would be a candidate for immunotherapy under those conditions. Dr. Damon would let me know about that, once he had seen the patient and reviewed his medical records.

Immunotherapy is biologic therapy and is designed to boost the body's natural defenses to fight the cancer. Genetic sequencing can be done with tissue obtained by biopsy, or after a lobe resection, to determine whether genetic mutations may exist. If so, drugs are developed to fight these mutations and are called targeted therapies. T-cells, an integral part of the immune system, has the job of attacking the cancer cells. However, some cancers develop a protein which tells the patient's T-cells to ignore the cancer. Some therapies work by blocking this cancer protein, which allow the T-cells to once again recognize the cancer cells and kill them.

I had a headache after reading for an hour and was once again glad I was a simple bone doctor. Deciding which immunotherapy would be best for poor Les was in the hands of Dr. Robert Damon, a man I respected much more after reading about lung-cancer treatment options.

I was dozing again when my pager went off. I dialed the number on the screen, and Dr. Ben Silverman answered.

"Hey, Ben. What's up?"

"I've arranged a settlement conference on the Howard Peck case for Tuesday afternoon at 5 p.m. Can you make it?"

"Yes. Are you sure you want me there? I'm not party to the lawsuit."

"I do. John Quinlan called me this afternoon and requested your presence. He thought you would be a somewhat impartial observer and would facilitate the matter at hand."

"I have clinic on Tuesday, so I should be done by then. Happy to help out, Ben."

"Just remember, Jim, that you're on the side of UMC and your fellow physicians."

"I'm well aware of that, Ben, but just remember that this case involves my uncle's untimely death due to the admitted negligence of staff physicians."

He paused, then said, "See you Tuesday."

CHAPTER 34

SETTLEMENT CONFERENCE

Monday, September 23, 2002

I was up at 5 a.m. on Monday and made rounds with the staff at 6 a.m., followed by a full surgery day. Tim Stacy, the fellow, was back at work. His wife's mother had come to town to help with their kids. His son with the fractured femur was doing great, too great perhaps, as Tim found him over the weekend on the swing set in their backyard using his good leg to catapult himself high in the air, while his two younger brothers played "sword battle" with the older boy's crutches.

Shelley's dad was recovering well, and in a twist of fate, his wife Liz had struck up a friendship with, of all people, Erik, Princess Sara's husband. They both were sitting in the lounge area of Abercrombie Pavilion Sunday afternoon awaiting teatime when they discovered each other reading the same magazine, *Horse and Rider*. It turns out the Comptons had a horse farm and raised polo ponies, Thoroughbreds, and Arabians. Erik's passion was raising the same breeds and playing polo. After a lengthy conversation, they became fast friends. It turned out Erik was not just a kept man, and good for him.

Monday's surgeries were uneventful, just how I like them, and Les Mimms's workup was in progress. I had spoken to Dr. Damon last Friday before I left for the settlement conference, and he was optimistic about immunotherapy treatment. He mentioned something about genetic markers and T-cells and checkpoint inhibitors and I basically went brain-dead. He thought he might be able to start the injections on Thursday. Les would have to be around for a week or two, then might be able to return to Fort Worth and complete the injections there, once the medications had been synthesized. It sounded like good news to me. Les was in good spirits on rounds Tuesday morning.

Tuesday afternoon at 5 p.m., I returned to the president's conference room, where I greeted Dr. Ben Silverman, Dr. Richard Damon, Dr. Joe Spears, Dr. Ed Crawford, and John Quinlan and his paralegal. The representative for UMC's insurance carrier joined the meeting via audio conferencing. Nothing could be accomplished or agreed to without his approval.

Ben began by welcoming us to the meeting, and he hoped that cooler heads would prevail during the discussions about Howard Peck.

"I don't have any business here," said Ed Crawford. "I shouldn't have been sued. I just do what the internists and oncologists want done. I'm the surgeon, not the diagnostician. I don't have the time to go over every scan and lab test on my patients. I would never get any work done. I have to take my colleagues' word for what the problem is, and then I go in and fix it."

"Dr. Crawford," said John Quinlan, "did you in fact perform, or partially perform, a liver transplant on Howard Peck? And did he in fact bleed to death during your operation?"

"Yes, but—"

"Then you have every reason to be here, sir, and I would appreciate your speaking when the time is appropriate for you to speak. We have an agenda, and we would like to keep our items to be discussed in order."

It was apparent to me that attorney Quinlan was in charge of the meeting and that we would be wise to shut our respective mouths and listen to his resolutions.

"UMC is one of the most respected institutions in Houston. Between the cancer hospital, Children's Hospital, the Cardiac Institute, and all those other divisions, you people perform great work. And I don't want to see that change, and I don't want its reputation to be tarnished. Hell, even I had my hip repaired by Jim Brady here. But mistakes have been made, and there will be repercussions.

"I'm going to summarize the important aspects of the case. Mr. Peck sought treatment for what his family doctor diagnosed as cirrhosis of the liver due to chronic alcoholism. He was sober for the last thirty years or so, but the damage had been done. He was sent to East Texas Medical Center in Tyler, where he was found to have cirrhosis, but also pancreatic cancer. The lesion was discovered on the PET scan but not seen on either CT or MRI scan. He was scheduled for treatment, but for reasons we don't know, he declined.

"He was referred to Dr. Damon at UMC by an ER doctor in Mr. Peck's hometown of Zavalla due to severe excoriation of his skin from itching due to elevated bilirubin, a liver enzyme. He was worked up here and was found to have cirrhosis and liver cancer. Total body scans did not reveal any metastases or any cancers outside the liver, so the decision was made to perform a liver transplant, which would be curative.

"Dr. Crawford performed the transplant, but during the procedure, the patient developed uncontrollable hemorrhaging and died, in spite of a magnanimous effort of the staff.

"Dr. Jeff Clarke from the pathology department discovered at autopsy that the cause of the hemorrhage was an undiagnosed pancreatic cancer, which had, at some point in time during the procedure, eroded into the superior mesenteric artery. Whether by some sort of manipulation by the surgeon during the procedure, or through an unfortunate quirk of fate, we'll never know.

"I have learned through a study of the medical records that the pancreatic cancer was not diagnosed here at UMC due to a delay in performance of the PET scan, allowing an apparent metabolism of the tracer medication prior to the scan being completed. In other words, the radioactive portion of the tracer was long gone before the scan began because it has a short half-life, and since the tumor was hidden in the pancreatic head back behind the liver and not seen on CT or MRI scan, the pancreatic cancer was missed.

"I think that sums it up, gentlemen? Any questions or comments before I continue?"

The room was eerily quiet, especially considering there were five type-A physicians and surgeons present.

"Good. Dr. Silverman and I have had a discussion about damages and the settlement terms and have come to an understanding. Each of you three physicians involved are employees of the University Medical Center, and therefore your malpractice premiums are paid by UMC. I've looked at the policies, and you each have $1,000,000/$3,000,000 coverage, meaning an individual occurrence of $1,000,000 and an aggregate of $3,000,000. Our agreement as of this time is for each of you to pay the max of the individual coverage, which would be $1,000,000 each, and thus a total of $3,000,000. UMC would then exercise their policy, which is a lot more than you three have, and put up an additional $5,000,000. That's a total of $8,000,000 to settle this case."

"That's preposterous," complained Ed Crawford. "This man was a preacher, for God's sakes. He didn't make much money, plus he had terminal cancer, with a predicted life span of maybe six months. His life isn't worth that kind of money!"

"So, Dr. Crawford, how do you judge what a man's life is worth?" Quinlan asked.

"Well, by how much money he's earned and what he's done for others. Look at me, for instance. I've been a surgeon for thirty years and have operated on thousands of patients and have cured many life-or-death problems. My life is certainly worth more than a preacher who was almost dead, don't you think?"

"We don't really need to have this discussion, Dr. Crawford, since as an employee of UMC, any settlements made on your behalf can be entrusted to Dr. Silverman and the board members of UMC without your approval. That said, we asked you here as a courtesy and to inform you of the plan to settle this lawsuit involving Howard Peck, a man that you clearly killed in the operating room. And that makes me wonder, Doctor, how many other patients you have killed over the years that found themselves in life-or-death situations. I personally would love to go back over the past five years of your medical records and see what I could find. But that's not going to happen. You're going to sign these documents and agree to allow your insurance company to pay $1,000,000 to the family of Howard Peck, and hope and pray to God that I don't get any more malpractice accusations against you, because I will make your life a living hell if I do."

"Any more questions or comments, Doctors?" asked Ben Silverman.

There were none.

"We have seven days to sign the documents," Ben said. "It's all or nothing, gentlemen. Either you all sign, or there is no deal, and Mr. Quinlan here will be free to declare open and public warfare against each of you and University Hospital. That is a sobering thought, and I strongly suggest you all put your egos aside and settle this case."

After the doctors departed, Silverman, Quinlan, and I remained.

"What's your fee, John, if I might ask?"

"Normally 40 percent, Jim Bob. It's called a contingency fee. We have agreed to pay expenses out of that sum, and I would call that fee the industry standard. Your aunt will receive $4.8 million, my firm will receive $3.2 million. There will be no court costs, for obvious reasons, and in case you didn't know, settlements from a personal injury negligence case are not taxable. Your Aunt Lela should be able to take care of herself, her two sons, their wives, and her five grandchildren just fine, with proper management of the funds."

He stood, shook our hands, and said "Good day, gentlemen."

Ben Silverman and I remained in the conference room.

"How do you think it went, Jim?"

"Probably better than expected, except for Ed Crawford. He's a loose cannon with an ego larger than most. Typical cardiovascular surgeon."

"What's your take on this missing woman, Theresa Banfield? Do you think there is anything there that would help us out in this case?"

"I don't know, Ben. It wouldn't hurt to check it out. You know my son has a PI firm, B&B Investigations. I can ask him to get right on it. He doesn't come cheap, but he will deliver quickly. Sounds like we have a week before all hell breaks loose. You probably know that Quinlan is a darling of the media. He gives a lot of money to various charities, and that smile of his has won many a jury verdict in his favor. We have everything to lose and nothing to gain by failing to settle this case, unless something about this mystery woman relates to the delayed PET-scan injection. I couldn't tell from Joe Spears's attitude at the meeting last week if he knew more than he let on. What do you think?"

"I haven't known him long enough to tell. Consider your son's firm hired."

CHAPTER 35

HUMAN RESOURCES

Wednesday, September 25, 2002

On Wednesday after surgery, I called attorney Tom O'Leary. I felt he deserved an update on my consideration of his proposal.

"Dr. Brady. Good to hear from you. Have you and your lovely wife decided to take the Sanderses' generous offer?"

"Tom, this may seem like a strange request, but I want to see for myself."

"See what?"

"The operation. The wells, the land, get a feel for what I would be the beneficiary of. I've never seen an operating well, except for those pump jacks—I think oil people call them grasshoppers—you see when you're driving the country roads in Texas."

"An odd request, but not totally out of order. Do you think it would be more or less likely to convince you to take this deal once you've seen the land and its operations?"

"No idea, Tom. I just need to see what's going on. Friday morning okay with you? I'm sure Mary Louise will want to go along. How long is the drive down to Cotulla? I'm thinking four hours or so."

He hesitated for a moment. "We'll take the Sanderses' Bell Jet Ranger helicopter. It's very handy to have, makes going back and forth from Houston to check on their properties easy. The trip will take one-and-a-half hours each way, and we can fly directly over the land and see it close up. You couldn't drive around and see 25,000 acres of land unless you had days to waste. You okay with heights?"

"J. J. on the back line," Frannie said, after my call to Tom O'Leary had ended.

"Hello, son. Any news on our missing X-ray tech?

"Not only no, Pop, but hell, no. Nothing, nada, zip. She doesn't exist."

"What?" I said, as I stood up out of my office chair.

"That's right. I talked to the radiology supervisor, who transferred me to human resources. I had authorization from Dr. Silverman to review her employment records. She has a portfolio of information, all bogus. Her social security number doesn't exist, her address is fraudulent, her phone number with AT&T is nonexistent. She has several letters of recommendation from previous employers at various hospitals and clinics around the Houston area. I tracked them all down, spoke to HR at those institutions, and they have no record of her employment. She's a ghost, Pop."

"Have you told Ben yet?"

"No, I wanted to talk to you first. This is my first time to strike out in searching for someone, and the situation reeks of intent to defraud. This is all about settling a malpractice claim, right?"

"Right, and all about my Uncle Howard. She's a key to the PET-scan fiasco he had, prior to the decision to perform a liver transplant. I explained that to you, right?"

"Yes, I remember. By any chance would there be a photo of her somewhere? We have some pretty sophisticated facial-recognition software. HR sent me a grainy photo via email. Any chance you could go there and get me a better copy? That's my last hope to try and identify this lady."

"I'll go now. Thanks."

I had Frannie call ahead so HR would expect me. I had to walk a couple of miles over the elevated walkways, and through a couple of hospitals, before finding their offices in the administration building. I spoke to a young lady at the desk, who escorted me to the supervisor's office.

"Afternoon, I'm Dr. Jim Brady. Tell me you have something we can use in the way of a photo."

She extended her hand. "Your reputation proceeds you, Doctor. My pleasure to meet you. I'm Carla Wellborn."

"My pleasure as well." She was petite and slim, with tortoiseshell glasses and short brown hair.

"I emailed a photo to your son, but apparently the resolution wasn't good enough for the facial-ID software he's using. This is all kind of exciting, isn't it? Intrigue at the UMC. Good fodder for a novel, wouldn't you think?"

"Maybe a short story, and a very short one at that, I hope."

She handed me the photo. I had seen this woman somewhere recently but couldn't remember where. She had disguised her looks somewhat, had maybe a different hair color, maybe glasses, but I still could recognize her face. Where the hell was it???

"May I keep the original? It's critical, and I'm sure Dr. Silverman would approve."

"He's already okayed your taking the original, Doctor. Good luck!"

"J. J., I have the original photo. I've seen this woman somewhere."

"What? You've got to be kidding."

"No, I just can't remember where. I'll take it home to your mom, maybe she was with me. You can stop by the apartment and pick it up later. You're welcome to stay for dinner."

"Do you recognize that face?" I asked Mary Louise. We were sitting at the kitchen island, sharing a Rombauer chardonnay.

"I admit she does look familiar. The hair is different, and those glasses distort her facial features, but I have seen her somewhere. We probably saw her together, since we both sort of recognize the face. Where have we been together lately?"

"Are you kidding? Everywhere! Restaurants, donor parties, the CCFA Ball. We went to Howard's funeral, burial service, and reception. We went to Fort Worth to see Les Mimms. We ate at the Stockyard Restaurant and walked around downtown Fort Worth. We've seen thousands of people in the past few weeks alone. It's like a needle in a haystack, trying to place this woman.

"I invited J. J. to dinner, by the way."

"I know, he called. I picked up Grotto takeout—caprese salad, fettucine Alfredo, chicken parmesan, linguini with clams, and Key lime pie."

I stared at her.

"What?"

"You're an amazing woman. Have I ever told you that?"

"Almost every day, but a girl likes to be complimented, and you can't hear that too often, as far as I'm concerned."

We had a nice dinner, just the three of us, like old times. I left J. J. to wash dishes with his mother and took Tipster down for his nightly

186 ACT OF ATONEMENT

stroll through the doggie park. There was another golden there, and after the requisite sniffing each other in the savory places, Tip got down to getting his business taken care of.

J. J. had gone home, photo in hand, when I returned. He said he would let me know something tomorrow, according to Mary Louise.

"We have a trip planned Friday morning and I hope you're available," I told her.

"Where to?"

"Cotulla, Texas."

"Whatever for?"

"I want to see the property where the wells were drilled. It's something I need to do. I can't tell you exactly why, just something I must do."

"I'm in. I can rearrange my schedule. That's quite a drive, isn't it?"

"O'Leary is taking us in a Bell Jet Ranger helicopter. Said an hour and a half each way. We can fly right over the land."

"How are you with heights?"

"That's what he asked."

CHAPTER 36

HELICOPTER RIDE

Friday, September 27, 2002

We met Tom O'Leary at West Houston Airport at 8 a.m. The morning was clear with no wind, ideal conditions, the pilot said when he introduced himself. We climbed into the Bell 206 Jet Ranger. Tom took the copilot seat, and Mary Louise and I buckled ourselves into the two jump seats behind. I looked down at my boots and was surprised to see that the aircraft had a Plexiglas floor. The pilot instructed us to put on the headphones, which we did, and he gave us a few preflight instructions, including all the things you're supposed to do if the aircraft is on fire or appears to be going to crash. This was of course disconcerting, but it was a typical preflight briefing that most all passengers ignore when a flight attendant explains the various exits and the oxygen masks that magically fall from the ceiling. I had no doubt that if this helicopter went down, we'd all be toast.

The pilot revved the engines, and suddenly we lifted off, initiating nausea on my part. I had to look away from the Plexiglas floor, finding that to be the instigator of the need to throw up breakfast. Looking out to the side wasn't so bad. I quickly understood why I had been asked about heights. I was dizzy as hell on the ascent. Mary Louise, however, was having a great time, mouthing WHEE as this spindly excuse for a flying vehicle gained speed in both a vertical and horizontal direction. My God, what had I gotten myself into? was my primary thought.

The chatty pilot told us we would be climbing to an altitude of 6500 feet and reach a cruising speed of 150 miles per hour. I looked out the side window and saw that we were following Interstate 10 west, passing over Columbus, Schulenburg, and Flatonia. East of San Antonio, the pilot made a sharp left turn and headed south, explaining that we were not allowed to penetrate the no-fly zones over the eighteen military bases there, including Lackland AFB and Fort Sam Houston.

The land below was flat and full of scrub oaks and mesquite trees—arid territory clearly, with little or no water visible. As we descended and the speed slowed, I began to see cows, farm buildings, ranch houses, and oil derricks, as well as pumpjacks.

O'Leary chimed in thru the headphones to say we were crossing over the northeastern border of Sanders property, the Double Eagle Ranch. We dropped down in altitude further to 1000 feet, then 500 feet, at which level the topography was clear. We zoomed around the ranch border, abruptly rising and falling at the pilot's whim, dodging telephone cables, power lines, and tall derricks drilling for oil. The land wasn't much to look at, and disappointment rose within me. I don't know what I had expected—lakes, giant oaks and elms, pastures of bright-green grass? There was none of that visible.

"There's your 100 acres, Doc, off to the right of the fuselage," said O'Leary. "A thing of beauty, huh?"

No, not really. The land had recently been excavated, with two pumpjacks located acres apart. Dirt was the primary commodity, interspersed with white caliche so that the various trucks that now serviced the wells wouldn't get stuck, or so O'Leary said. It looked to me like this area of the ranch hadn't seen rain in years, so why bother with the caliche?

We were low enough in altitude to see a Southern Natural Gas truck pull up to a strange contraption constructed of various pipes, spools, fittings, and gauges, away from the pumpjacks but in the same locale.

"What's the truck doing?" I asked.

"Servicing the Christmas tree," said O'Leary. "The tree is used to regulate the flow of well fluids and gas coming from the ground. It is very important to keep that baby in perfect working order. Otherwise, a lot of production revenue is lost."

We passed over a multitude of cows, goats, and horses, all contained within pastures surrounded by white four-board fencing. We saw farm equipment scattered about, small houses, larger houses, and an enormous ranch-style home that probably represented the owners' abode.

We circled back around the small plot of stripped Brady-owned land, then suddenly rose a few thousand feet, leaving my stomach back at five hundred feet. "What's the fuel consumption in the helicopter?" I asked.

"If you're asking how long we can stay aloft," said the pilot, "about three hours without refueling. Why?"

"I was wondering how far out of the way it would be to fly over Granite Falls."

"That would add at least thirty minutes, maybe more, to the flight home. I'd feel safer if we refueled there."

"Why Granite Falls, Doc?" asked O'Leary.

"Mary Louise and I have heard about Lake LBJ and the pretty little towns around it, but we haven't been there. I thought this might be a good time, since we're in this Bell Jet Ranger and we could take in a lot of scenery in a short time. Of course, if it's too much trouble—"

"No, no trouble at all," said O'Leary. He gave the pilot instructions, and he in turn changed the aircraft's direction to north, ratcheted up the speed, and off we went.

I had done some reading about the area. Named after President Lyndon B. Johnson, Lake LBJ is part of the Highland Lakes chain of seven lakes starting in Austin and going northwest for eighty-five miles. Lake LBJ starts near Horseshoe Bay, fifty miles from Austin, and goes all the way to Kingsland. It's a constant-level lake extending over twenty-one miles and is said to be perfect for sailing, boating, fishing, and all other water-related activities.

I must have dozed off, because Mary Louise was tapping my thigh. "Huh?"

"We're here. Take a look."

If I had to describe the scenery with one word, it would be "spectacular." The lakes were clearly visible; it was still a cloudless day, fortunately, and the dams between the various pristine bodies of water on the Colorado River were well defined. We flew over the small towns of Marble Falls, Kingsland, Granite Shoals, Horseshoe Bay, and Granite Falls. There wasn't much traffic, a major plus, but the lakes were dotted with small sailboats, fishing boats, Jet Skis, and pontoon boats. We were low enough to see the golf courses; I counted four.

The pilot decided to refuel at a tiny airport in Horseshoe Bay. We deplaned, stretched our legs, and breathed in the clean, fresh air that we were not used to, living in Houston, auto-exhaust capital of Texas.

"Feels pretty good to me, Mary Louise. How about you?"

"I could get used to a lifestyle change, darlin'. Probably a little slower pace over here, huh?"

"Yep. Still, only an hour from Austin and three-and-a-half hours from Houston, if we started missing traffic, crime, and pollution."

"Why don't you take some time off, rent something here on or near the water, and see how we like it? Maybe a couple of weeks?"

"Sounds good to me."

"Are you swayed toward taking the Sanders' offer now?"

"Yep."

CHAPTER 37

B & B

Friday, September 27, 2002

We arrived back in Houston around noon, thanked our hosts for the ride, and assured Tom O'Leary we would be in touch soon. I told the pilot to let me know if he found my stomach when he cleaned up the airplane, and to FedEx it to me. I would not be found enjoying a helicopter ride again any time soon.

Mary Louise and I headed east on Westheimer Road in search of Mexican food. It was Friday, after all, and I was off for the weekend. We stopped at Guadalajara's and ordered margaritas royale from a somewhat private booth in the rear of the restaurant.

"Have you heard any more from J. J. about the missing X-ray tech?" Mary Louise asked.

"Let me look at my phone. I forgot to check messages."

I scrolled down the list of calls and messages, saw one from B&B, and opened it. All it read was "Bingo," with a message saved.

I nodded, returned his call rather than listening to the message, and put him on speakerphone so Mary Louise could also hear his comments.

"Hey, Pops, we have several matches on the facial-recognition software. I can't imagine how you would be in contact with some of these people, since both you and Mom said you recognized Theresa

Banfield's face. Some of these folks are miscreants, felons even, and ex-cons. There were four left once I discarded all the unlikely players, so here's what we have.

"Brenda Lane, age forty-three, former nurse at University Medical Center, small-time criminal and part-time drug dealer. She was convicted of selling opioids to other nurses and residents on the neurology floor where she worked. She's been out of jail for almost a year, clean and sober, it looks like. She lost her nursing license because of the conviction and now works in housekeeping at University General. Sound familiar?"

"Not at all, son. Sounds like Nurse Jackie from the TV series."

"Right. Next is Joyce Lange, no criminal convictions, currently a laboratory technician at UMC. I thought she might be a patient of yours, or maybe you had come in contact with her in one of your 'snooping around' mysteries."

"Doesn't sound familiar."

"Next is your own Fran Makowski."

"My secretary of twenty years??? You're kidding."

"Think about it. Her features are similar, if you change the hair and add glasses. Remember, I'm trying to match facial-recognition software with women working in the medical field, preferably UMC, that you might have come in contact with."

"Forget Fran."

"Fine. Lastly there is a woman that I guess it's possible you and Mom may have both come in contact with, and I only flagged her because of a familiar last name. She lived in Oklahoma City at one time and has worked as a radiology technician in the past, but never in Houston, according to my records. Her name is Tammy Peck. Ring a bell?"

Mary Louise and I stared at each other. "Holy shit," I said. "Isn't that one of Uncle Howard's boys' wives?"

"Yes. I think she's Ron's wife, the preacher's wife. What was Rico's wife's name? Let me think . . . Gloria, I believe. We only saw them the one time, at the reception after Howard's funeral. What in the world?"

"J. J., thanks much. Our food just arrived. Let me call you back after we eat."

Mary Louise drove home while I made some calls. My first was to Carla Wellborn, human resources supervisor at UMC.

"What a pleasant surprise, Dr. Brady. What can I do for you?"

"Strange question, I'm sure, but when you hire someone to work at UMC, do you take a DNA sample or fingerprint the individual?"

When she stopped laughing, she said, "Of course not. That policy would violate a ton of privacy laws."

"I'm sure it would, Carla. Let me ask you this, and I would appreciate your confidentiality regarding our attempt to discover the real identity of this Theresa Banfield. If you hire an employee to work anywhere in the system, and let's say that individual is up to nefarious activities and provides all the information you require—past employment history, social security number, current address and phone—and it's all bogus, how would one be able to prove that the employee had committed said acts without some sort of physical proof such as DNA or a fingerprint match?"

"You can't, unless the employee confesses to the crime. By the way, that happened once before. An employee with what turned out to be bogus credentials was accused of theft. Without DNA or fingerprint evidence, she simply denied it, and without corroborating evidence, she was fired because of the credentials issue, but she walked away a free woman. I wanted to start fingerprinting all employees after that nasty episode, but the lawyers said absolutely not. We know we're supposed to check the credentials of potential employees, but in a system this big, we often just don't have the time or the personnel.

"I'm sorry you find yourself in this situation, Dr. Brady, but unless there is a criminal complaint and physical evidence of some sort is left behind to compare to the perpetrator, there is no case. We would fire her, of course, if she ever returned, because of the bogus credentials."

I called Susan Beeson next, one of Mary Louise's best friends, a detective and the daughter of HPD's chief of police.

"Dr. Brady, I presume? How are you?"

"Great, thanks. You and the family?"

"Excellent, thank you."

"And the old man?" Her dad, Stan Lombardo, as well as being the chief of police, was a former patient of mine.

"Complaining as usual. What can I do for you?"

I went through the whole rigmarole with her, beginning with the delayed isotope injection for the PET scan, to the disappearance of the nonexistent Theresa Banfield, to the discovery of the possibility that my first cousin's wife, and a preacher's wife at that, may in fact be the guilty party. I discussed the DNA and fingerprint issue with her and asked her opinion about what the next step should be.

"I don't think this is a police matter, Jim Bob. You have a dead patient who was going to die soon anyway, a lawsuit about a missed cancer diagnosis that may or may not have influenced the outcome but that would benefit the family of the deceased, and a suggestion that the patient's own daughter-in-law may have been responsible, although there is no DNA nor fingerprint data to confirm that. The only possible crime HPD could charge her with is impersonating an employee of the hospital, although technically, using her false credentials, she was in fact just an employee who walked off the job. It sounds like a family mess to me, and I would recommend HPD steer clear of this matter. Certainly there is no evidence of a capital crime, at least one that could be proven.

"My advice to you is to confront the woman, see if she'll confess to her misdeeds, and get some closure for yourself. Otherwise, I think you all are stuck with the outcome, including the lawsuit."

CHAPTER 38

ZAVALLA, TEXAS

Friday, September 27, 2002

I called my mother late Friday afternoon and told her I needed to meet with Aunt Lela Belle, Ron, Rico, and their wives on Saturday regarding a settlement in the lawsuit they had filed, and I asked her if she could facilitate that. She returned my call later that evening, confirmed that yes, she'd spoken with everyone and a family meeting was possible with the group Saturday afternoon at Aunt Lela's house in Zavalla.

I asked Mary Louise to make the trek with me, her being of sound mind and much more pleasant to deal with than I. She would be an ideal buffer between me and my relatives, who certainly would prefer M. L. to me in pretty much any circumstance.

We left at nine in the morning and took Highway 69 into Livingston, then Highway 190 east into Woodville, then Highway 69 north into the thriving metropolis of Zavalla, population 662. The 135-mile trip took two hours. As far as I could tell, the only attraction in the town was Sam Rayburn Lake, only a few minutes away from "downtown." Mary Louise and I found a small diner on the lake and had an early lunch of fried catfish, fried okra, and hush puppies with cream gravy. I could have used a beer or two but thought I would try and keep my wits about me and had a soda instead.

We had a little trouble finding the place, seeing as how the address was on a Farm Market Road which wasn't marked with signage of any kind. M. L. studied the map and eventually had me turn down a gravel road, wander between some giant oaks and elms, and dodge some chickens, then finally we reached a clearing. On the property sat an old clapboard one-story house in need of paint, with several cars scattered in the yard. There was a detached garage off to the side, housing two fairly recent-model cars, both American made.

People started out the front door as soon as we pulled up, along with a few barking dogs who ran at us like they had never seen town people before. We deflected them deftly and managed to keep them from knocking us over. I didn't hear anyone try and stop the dogs from jumping on us, so I assumed this was the alarm system for the house, and we were considered outsiders. No surprise there.

"Aunt Lela, you remember Mary Louise?"

"Of course." Lela tried to shake my wife's hand, but M. L. artfully took her hand and turned it into a hug.

Ron and Rico were both there, along with their wives. The men shook hands.

"It's Tammy, right?" I said to Ron's mate.

"Yes, nice to see you again," she said. I looked her over closely and saw a blond mane with blue eyes. No glasses, no brown hair. She was trim, but not thin. This girl looked nothing like the photo of employee Theresa Banfield, who in the photo had brown hair, brown eyes, and glasses, and was skinny.

"I'm a hugger," Gloria said, as she grabbed both Mary Louise and me into a strong grip. I remembered her from the funeral and reception, but no gold jewelry was evident today. She had blond hair as well, with a few black streaks. She was a little on the heavy side, as well as full in the chest and hips.

Ron the preacher shook my hand. He was fair, slim, and good-looking in a . . . well, in a preacher sort of way. His hair was combed into a pompadour, a popular hairstyle for many men of the cloth in our neck of the woods.

Rico the pawn-shop owner was shorter, heavy, wore thick glasses, and looked none too friendly.

"I've made some tea," Aunt Lela said, a signal for all of us to come inside and sit down and act like we were there for a pleasant family gathering. She was gaunt, had dark circles under her eyes, and wore a loose faded housedress.

After everyone accepted sweet tea in paper cups, I started the conversation. "As you all know, I'm acting as a mediator in the lawsuit discussion between you, John Quinlan, and University Hospital. The lawsuit centers on the misdiagnosis of Uncle Howard's pancreatic cancer. It was missed during his evaluation at UMC due to a technicality, really, a delayed scan for the isotope for his PET scan. This rendered the PET-scan results invalid by failing to reveal the pancreatic tumor. Had the doctors at UMC seen this lesion, when combined with the liver cancer and cirrhosis, they would NOT have recommended he have the liver transplant. But, because of this isotope issue, if you will, the lesion was not seen, the transplant was performed, and Uncle Howard bled to death during the procedure.

"Looking back over his treatment, both at UMC and at East Texas Medical Center, I'm curious as to why none of you ever mentioned to me or anyone else at UMC that the doctors at East Texas had found pancreatic cancer and had rejected him for a liver transplant because of that."

They all stared at each other. Ron spoke, apparently the spokesperson for the family. "We didn't really understand there were two different cancers, I guess. The East Texas doctors talked about the 'cancer,' the UMC doctors talked about the 'cancer,' so we all thought they were talking about the same cancer. We're not medical people, you know."

"From what I've been told, Tammy has been trained in X-ray technology, so she has some idea about medicine and cancer treatment and certainly would be well-versed in some of the testing that goes on."

I saw a lot of collective head shaking.

"Tammy was an X-ray tech years ago, but after we got married and had children, she gave it up to stay home," answered Ron.

"Tammy, you haven't worked in a long time?"

"No, sir," she said, eyes averted.

"Why didn't Howard opt for treatment for his pancreatic cancer at East Texas?" I asked.

Ron answered. "Because they told him his liver was shot with cirrhosis, and that because of the location of the cancer, all they could offer him was radiotherapy and chemotherapy, and that the chemotherapy would probably not work because it's metabolized in the liver and his liver had too much disease. Essentially the docs gave him a death sentence of six months, so he just decided to go home and die without treatment.

"Then, when Mom took him to the Zavalla clinic for severe itching, and the doctor arranged a transfer for him to UMC in Houston, and the doctors started talking about how he was able to have a liver transplant after all, we got our hopes up and figured they knew what they were talking about. And you had seen Dad, and talked with him, and talked with the doctors, and you seemed to agree with their plan, so we thought, right on, let's 'git her done.'"

And there it was, the glaring mistake *I* had made, supporting the liver transplant with inadequate information. I, like the rest of Howard's family, accepted the treating physicians' words and didn't try and stop the proceedings. In fact, as I remember, I treated the whole episode in a cavalier fashion, not wanting to be bothered with the trials and tribulations of my late uncle. I only seemed to get seriously involved AFTER his death, in an attempt to carry out his final wishes and locate Bull and make amends. Maybe that was guilt on my part, although I didn't realize it at the time.

"We're very close to a settlement in your case. The doctors have until Tuesday or Wednesday to sign off on it. It would involve the insurance company for each of the three doctors putting up $1,000,000, and UMC putting up $5,000,000, for a total of $8,000,000. You would get 60 percent of that, Lela, for a total of $4,800,000. The rest goes to the attorney, Mr. Quinlan. An important fact to remember is that the law firm has agreed to pay all the expenses out of their settlement portion. Your money is free and clear, Lela, since taxes are not paid on personal-injury settlements. I think you and your family would be well-fixed with that kind of money."

They stared at each other, nodded in turn.

"I want you all to know something, and that this discussion is between us and ends with me here today. Mary Louise and I made this trip to visit with you, and for me to close the chapter on Uncle Howard. You all know that I had the task of finding an old friend of your dad's, Les Mimms? He related to me the night before his operation that he never told you all about Les. That right?"

They looked at each other, shook their heads.

"Well, he traveled the rails with your dad, back in the old wino days when they were both being chased by their respective demons. I realize Howard was gone off and on for years, a hardship for Lela and you two boys. I don't know what your family life was like after he returned home, but I doubt the adjustment was easy. The night before his surgery, he asked me to find his old buddy"—I saw no reason at this point to mention that Howard thought he had killed said buddy—"because he wanted to make amends. I did find his friend, who ironically has lung cancer, and I've arranged for him to now be treated at UMC. I don't know whether that goes some way toward helping to make amends on Howard's behalf. But I think Howard also wanted to make amends to you as well. Maybe that's what this lawsuit is all about, making amends to you for all those years he was gone. Giving you a financial windfall to give your family a better life.

"I can't prove it, but I have a strong feeling that somehow Tammy got herself recertified in X-ray technology and got hired at UMC under the name of Theresa Banfield, all for the said purpose of an elaborate scheme to falsify the PET-scan results. I think Howard had figured out the plan, and that you all knew what was going on and were part of the scheme to literally extort money from the hospital and the doctors through an ingenious malpractice lawsuit. That's the only route through this circuitous highway that explains all the happenings.

"But like I said, I can't prove it. There are no fingerprints on file, nor a DNA sample on this Theresa Banfield that can be compared to Tammy Peck. I've looked at all the angles and consulted a professional, and it just can't be proven. So, if I'm right, you've all gotten away with what appears to be Howard's incredible plan to make amends to you for his failures as a husband and father. That's my opinion."

Ron looked at me, then the others. "Well, Jim Bob, opinions are like assholes. Everybody has one."

CHAPTER 39

STORM

Wednesday, October 2, 2002

The rest of the weekend was quiet, as were the first few days of the following workweek, except for a tropical storm that was brewing in the Gulf of Mexico. The weather folks were predicting that it might become a hurricane but couldn't prognosticate further until forty-eight hours had passed. That would put the storm on land around Friday afternoon. In my experience, tropical storms had done almost as much damage as hurricanes during my tenure of more than thirty years in Houston. We Houstonians had learned, however, that one couldn't be too careful, so most of us erred on the side of caution. Friday would be a good day for workers to call in sick, if at all possible. That did not apply, of course, to the front-liners: police, firefighters, and EMTs.

Wednesday evening, over a homemade dinner of ground-beef tacos, Mary Louise broached the subject of the Reverend Roger Tuttle. He was an evangelist and a former faith healer who had become quite wealthy from donations he had received to heal folks of their various maladies, and he was a favored personality about town. He appeared on the talk shows often and was quite a personality, with his slicked-back hair, custom-made suits, and handsome features. His attendance at charity dinners was the dream of every charity-dinner organizer, including Mary Louise, as I was disconcerted to discover over dinner.

"There have been a lot of preachers over the years that have alleged themselves to be faith healers, only to discover that sins of the flesh conquered their souls and brought them down. Jim and Tammy Faye Bakker and Jimmy Swaggart come to mind. Oral Roberts originally was a faith healer but became a more traditional member of the Methodist church, I think, sometime after he started his college in Tulsa, and ended up respectable and a part of mainstream religion. Seems to me most of those preachers are shysters. Why would you care about this Roger Tuttle fellow?"

"Reverend Tuttle sits on the March of Dimes board, and the chairperson told me that Roger had mentioned to him that he wanted to give a substantial gift to the children's hospital or to the oncology hospital at UMC. He couldn't decide which and was asking the chairperson's advice."

"What did the chairperson say?" I asked, my interest piqued.

"He suggested Roger take a tour of the facilities and spend a few hours observing and interacting with patients in both sections of UMC, and that would probably lead him in the right direction for his donation."

"This is sounding like an adventure you want me get involved in."

"Well, since I'm on the MOD board, and you're on the staff of University Orthopedic Hospital, what better couple to interact with Roger and give him a tour of the facilities? We could invite the chief of pediatrics and the chief of oncology, and perhaps the president and CEO of University Hospital."

"When were you thinking about doing this, M. L.?"

"Friday afternoon, since you usually have most of the day off."

I stared at her in disbelief. "You mean this Friday, day of the tropical storm or possible hurricane landfall?"

"Yes. You know those weather people; they have the only job where you can be wrong half the time and still be employed."

"Funny. Still, I'm worried—"

"We'll be indoors, silly, and the only worry would be driving back and forth from home, fifteen minutes away. Worse comes to worst, we can stay in the Marriott if the weather gets bad. We can take a walkway directly there without going outside. It might even lead to romance," she said. "You just never know."

She batted her eyes at me when she said that. She made it sound so sweet and innocent, who could refuse an offer like that, especially with the thought of possible romance? I'm a sucker for the romance thing.

Thursday came and went, and on Friday morning I made rounds with Tim and Shelley and tied up loose ends. Shelley's dad was over the hump and doing well. Princess Sara was going gangbusters on the crutches and starting to talk about returning home to Tamborinia. Les Mimms had begun his custom-made immunotherapy cocktails and was expectant of a recovery. All the other patients were either going home, going to rehab, or hunkering down for the weekend, glad to be out of the weather and the horrendous traffic that tropical storms produced.

We met Roger Tuttle and his entourage at two in the afternoon at the conference center in the president/CEO's office, a room I had become familiar with recently with the litigation business. Introductions were made, and the tour began at Children's Hospital. The chief met us there and took Silverman, Mary Louise, Roger Tuttle and his entourage, and me to one of the floors where the affected children were housed. The March of Dimes was founded by President Franklin D. Roosevelt to combat polio, himself a victim. Once polio was virtually eliminated by the vaccine, the organization worked to prevent infant death and birth defects through education and genetic research. The children we visited that afternoon had disorders and disabilities that would break your heart. Absent arms, absent and deformed legs, and spinal deformities were abundant. Some of the kids were ambulatory with crutches and walkers, some motored along in wheelchairs. The most astounding thing I found was that the children were for the most part smiling and affable, and they joked about their own disabilities. It was all I could do to maintain decorum.

We finally left there after an hour and a half and headed to the oncology hospital. Passing through the second-floor walkways, I noticed the sky was dark, rain was pounding the Plexiglas walls, and the few trees on Fannin were leaning hard to the north. A tropical storm or worse was coming. I stepped to the side, called the Marriott, and confirmed the reservation I had booked on Wednesday as a precaution.

The patients at oncology were not so joyous as the children back at Children's Hospital. Mostly adults, they were all in various stages of treatment with either surgery, radiotherapy, chemotherapy, or some combination of the three. Then, to my amazement, the group wandered into Les Mimms's room. I introduced Les to the visitors. He shook everyone's hand, then held on to Roger Tuttle's grip. Roger leaned down to speak privately to Les. About that time, a clap of thunder broke the quiet. The storm was near, if not overhead.

Roger continued speaking to Les, and Les nodded. Roger put both hands around Les's face and started praying aloud. Those of us not in the evangelist's entourage looked at each other and wondered what was going on. Roger's praying became louder, and the last words I heard him say were "in the Name of the Lord Jesus Christ, be healed," and then the loudest clap of thunder I had ever heard boomed, and the lights flickered, then went out. There was absolute silence for a moment, then the thump of the generator activating, and dim lights began returning. After another minute or so, the lights flickered back on to full strength.

A nurse came into the room and asked if everyone was all right. We collectively said yes, and we watched as Roger Tuttle shook Les's hand and exited the room.

We followed the entourage back to the UMC conference center and said our goodbyes. By then it was after 5 p.m., and a powerful thirst arose.

"Let's get a drink at the Marriott. I booked a room just in case."

"Good idea. The weather looks hideous," Mary Louise said, and I agreed as I watched the water on Fannin Street rush over the curb onto the sidewalk. Cars suddenly were floating, all steering lost, and multiple crashes occurred simultaneously.

Seated at the bar, dirty martinis in hand, I asked, "What in the hell was that with Les Mimms?"

"I don't think it was anything to do with hell, Jim Bob. Looked like an attempt at faith healing to me."

"I haven't seen anything like that since I was a kid, when I used to hide under the pews in my mother's church after hearing parishioners speak in tongues and watching them fall into the aisles. I was honestly looking for a bed to hide under."

She laughed, said, "Poor baby," and patted my cheek.

We finished our cocktails and checked into what was termed a luxury room on the top floor, glad we had the foresight to make a reservation in order to enjoy the hotel for the evening.

We rode the elevator arm-in-arm. Suddenly I remembered our poor dog. "Mary Louise, what about Tip?" I said, panicked.

"Tonita is staying at the house for a day or two. He's just fine."

"Oh man, I can't believe I'm starting to forget something that important. Glad you didn't. How did you decide to have her stay at the house?"

"Girl Scouts—always be prepared. I would never forget about your second-best friend.

"And, thanks so much for doing the tour with Reverend Tuttle today. I know it's not your thing."

"You mean going to faith-healing revivals?"

"No, arranging a big show for dignitaries, silly. One of the institutions here will be the beneficiary of Reverend Tuttle's largesse, so everyone wins."

I located the room, used the key card, and entered.

"Nice digs," Mary Louise said, as she opened the thick drapes over the windows. "Funny how the storm looks beautiful from the fifteenth floor, but not so on the ground. By the way, I have bad news for you."

"What's that?"

"I didn't foresee the storm, and I have no nighties, so I'll have to sleep in the nude."

I wished I could get that kind of bad news all the time.

CHAPTER 40

AMENDS

October–November, 2002

It took over a month for the city to return to normal after the latest Texas flood, like the Stevie Ray Vaughan song. The stalled and flooded cars were towed away, the streets and storefronts cleaned of debris, and those folks living in low-lying areas called the 100-year flood plain vowed once again to move to higher ground. It rarely ever happened, the moving part, for reasons I don't completely understand, but most folks seemed reluctant to leave their home, regardless of the consequences.

As for the Bradys, we were able to get home Sunday, out of our house for only two days. Tip acted as though we had been gone for weeks, just about peeing himself, he was so excited to see us.

Princess Sara made a spectacular recovery, going after physical therapy for her hip replacement like a long-distance runner. On her last day at the hospital, I came to say goodbye and noticed she'd had candy and flowers delivered to all the staff at Abercrombie Pavilion, including the physical therapy workers. I don't think that Sara cares about the customs in Tamborinia regarding touching royals, because she hugged every person on duty that morning, including the house-keeping staff.

Erik was a little more reserved, nodding at the staff and walking away to the elevator bank with the valet, loaded with suitcases and boxes on a rolling cart.

"Well, Doctor, I guess this is goodbye," Sara said, as I made rounds for the last time with her in the hospital. "It was such a pleasure to get to know you, and I want to thank you for the outstanding care you rendered to me during my stay. I would love to see you again, so if you're in the neighborhood . . ."

"Sara, you were a wonderful patient, and I would be honored to take care of you any time, except I most likely won't be making the trip to your homeland. I'm sure you understand."

"Oh yes, Doctor, I do. Those of us in the royal family get out of there as often as possible."

She hugged me, gave me a chaste kiss on the cheek, and joined her husband. Erik did shake my hand, although reluctantly, and nodded a farewell.

Tim Stacy's son made a remarkable recovery after his femur fracture, which healed completely in a record time of twelve weeks. Prior to this case, the pediatric surgeon, Joe Frank Bennett, had kept his patients non-weight-bearing for six weeks. The young man apparently had a high pain threshold and started walking on the tiptoes of his injured extremity on the third day after surgery. Joe was now considering changing his protocol for postoperative care to include early weight-bearing, thinking that perhaps, if the fracture is stable from the rod insertion, weight-bearing might *facilitate* the healing, rather than the reverse. He had already begun a patient study on the matter and hoped to publish the results in *Pediatric Ortho* next year.

Tim was back at work full time and was, to his delight, able to send his mother-in-law back to her home.

Shelley Compton's dad left the hospital a week after his fracture surgery and went to a rehab facility for a couple of weeks. Once Liz got him home, however, she quickly realized that converting the dining room on the first level to a bedroom for her husband as a temporary measure was not cutting it—the problems of having a large house with sleeping quarters on the second and third floors—and shortly thereafter, she put the house on the market. They would be moving to a high-rise, where, as she put it, old folks belong.

Mary Louise learned at a recent March of Dimes board meeting that the Reverend Roger Tuttle had decided to give $5 million through his personal charity, the Heavenly Light Foundation, to Children's Hospital. Negotiations were apparently underway to determine how the gift was going to be used, and how Reverend Tuttle's name would be incorporated into the resulting entity established by the gift.

I had spoken to John Quinlan, who informed me that the settlement between Lela Peck and UMC had been concluded. Her check had been delivered and deposited. The settlement sum to her was $5.6 million dollars.

"John," I had asked, "that's higher than what you discussed at the settlement conference. I thought her portion was $4.8 million."

"Brady, I decided to give her the family discount and reduce my contingency fee from 40 percent down to 30 percent, seeing as how you and I are such good buddies. And because you wise folks at the hospital decided to settle quickly, expenses were minimal."

"Well, John, that's mighty kind of you. That's a lot of money for someone who's been living on a preacher's salary for thirty years. I hope she can manage that money well and not go too crazy with spending, like some of the lottery winners do."

"I gave her the same speech that I give all my clients who are awarded large settlement verdicts, and I included a referral to an excellent and honest money-manager acquaintance of mine. That's all I can do."

"I had this crazy dream a while back that she was driving around town in a Rolls-Royce."

"That can't happen, Brady, because you can't get service on a Rolls in Zavalla, Texas."

"Well, that makes me feel better. Listen, thanks again for all your work. I never cease to be amazed at these settlement verdicts you get, and how much money these contingency fees add up to. I spend at least fifty to sixty hours a week working my butt off, seeing patients in clinic, operating on folks and taking care of them, and I earn a drop in the bucket compared to your numbers. Makes me think I wasn't as smart as I thought I was when I went into medicine."

"Jim Bob, a mentor of mine once gave me some valuable advice early on in life, and it's served me well. He said, 'It's not the amount of time you spend, it's how you spend the time.' Until next time, my friend."

That motto of his was a thought provoker, and after pondering it for a week or so, I called Tom O'Leary to tell him I didn't feel it necessary to have his payout numbers audited. I would accept the most generous offer from him and the Sanders family. Three days later, a package was delivered to my office after clinic was done, and inside was the cashier's check for $16,162,414. I signed the accompanying papers agreeing to the settlement and handed the packet back to the messenger for immediate return to Tom O'Leary's office. We had our own messenger standing by, and after endorsing the check and writing DEPOSIT ONLY on the back, I placed it in an envelope and handed it to the messenger for immediate delivery to my banker, who was standing by to deposit my newly found fortune. I was still amazed at the recent developments that would change my life forever.

Les Mimms stayed at UMC for another week, getting his custom-concocted medications in order and making sure there were no side effects. He contacted his former oncologist in Fort Worth, who agreed to administer the medications as instructed by Dr. Robert Damon, his oncologist at UMC. He would have two injections per week and blood work done after, attention primarily being paid to the cancer markers.

Cancer markers are chemicals made by tumor cells, or made by normal cells in response to the cancer, that can be detected in a blood sample. Measuring the level of these markers is an indicator of how the cancer is responding to treatment. Each time Les received an infusion of the immunotherapy drugs, he had blood drawn to measure the cancer markers.

Dr. Robert Damon called me a few days ago to give me some startling news.

"Jim Bob, I'm puzzled by the test results I've been receiving from the oncologist in Fort Worth regarding Les Mimms."

"You mean bad puzzled, or good puzzled?"

"Well, good I guess, but I just can't understand these cancer-marker values I'm seeing. They are low. So low, in fact, that it's like cancer does not now exist, nor has it ever existed in this patient. It's virtually impossible for that to occur, especially in a stage-4 lung-cancer patient. This is either the most miraculous immunotherapy result I have ever seen in my career, or we witnessed some sort of cataclysmic cure in his hospital room a month ago during the Reverend Roger Tuttle tour. I'm not much of a religious man, Jim, but I'm at a loss for a reasonable explanation."

"Do you mean it's not possible that the immunotherapy could produce a result like this?"

"I didn't say that. What I said was that I've never seen it before, and I've contacted a dozen of my colleagues around the country, and no one has seen anything like this before."

"What's your plan, Robert?"

"Keep up the injections, continue to look at the cancer markers, and complete the prescribed course of treatment. That's all I know to do at this point."

"What are the chances of an exacerbation or a recurrence?"

"I have no idea, Jim. This one's uncharted, and I'm flying by the seat of my pants. I'll keep you posted of any changes, but as of now, Mr. Mimms is cured of lung cancer."

Mary Louise and I were sitting on the balcony on a fairly windless night, and again we were discussing ad nauseum both the Lester Mimms business and the Lela Peck business at length. They seemed to us both to be intertwined. Howard Peck saw me the night before his operation, told me he wanted to make amends, and implored me to carry out his wishes should he not, as he put it, see seventy-three years of age. At the time, I concentrated on finding the family of his old friend Bull in an effort to make amends for my uncle. However, I was not so sure that was the extent of Howard's wishes, and Mary Louise agreed. Yes, he had accidentally shot his best friend, and I had spent a great deal of time discovering his friend's identity and whereabouts, but that might not have been enough.

"Remember, your Uncle Howard had wandered on the rails for years, often drunk, having abandoned his wife and sons and leaving them to fend for themselves until he returned home at the age of forty-three or so," Mary Louise reminded me.

"He quit drinking, became a preacher, and started making amends for his errant ways. But maybe that was, in Howard's mind, insufficient."

"I agree with you, Mary Louise, and I believe he orchestrated his own death in such a way as to benefit the family, using his daughter-in-law Tammy's skills, with all family members complicit in the arrangement. But I can't prove it."

I returned to the kitchen and refilled our glasses of Rombauer chardonnay, almost tripping over Tip during the process.

"When Howard told me he wanted to make amends, maybe it wasn't just to Les Mimms's family—ultimately, to Les Mimms himself—but to Lela and his sons as well. And look what has transpired. Les is apparently cured of lung cancer, and Lela and her sons have gained an amount of wealth that will allow them and future generations of Pecks to live very comfortable lives."

"I agree with all you have surmised, husband. But don't make yourself crazy pondering all these developments. There is no proof for any of your conjectures, no matter how logical they might seem."

"You're correct, but I guess I'm destined to lose sleep over the mysteries surrounding my uncle's demise, at least for a while."

"Or until the next good mystery comes along that grabs your attention."

"That's probably true, Mary Louise, but one thing I do know for certain, and that is that my dear departed Uncle Howard Peck had made multiple acts of atonement . . . to everyone in his life that mattered to him."

And with that, we clinked our glasses to Uncle Howard, may he rest in peace.

THE END

READ ON FOR A SNEAK PEEK OF ACT OF MERCY

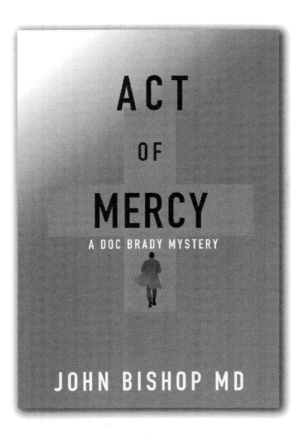

I hope you have enjoyed *Act of Atonement*, the sixth book in the Doc Brady Mystery series. I'm pleased to present you with a sneak peek of *Act of Mercy*, the seventh book.

Please visit **JohnBishopAuthor.com** to learn more.

CHAPTER 1

HILL COUNTRY MEDICAL CENTER

I entered the lobby of the Hill Country Medical Center through automatic sliding-glass doors; at least, they looked like glass to me. Could be Plexiglas, or some sort of artificial glass that was advertised to be unbreakable or break resistant. I wondered, with wheelchairs and walkers and probably stretchers passing through those doors daily, if there wasn't a hazard for making a mess with forceful contact. Glass everywhere, cuts and lacerations of a patient or visitor . . . that could get ugly. Although, in this beautiful small Hill Country town called Granite Falls, perhaps the mental wiring of individuals was different from that which I experienced living and practicing orthopedic surgery in Houston for thirty years. Maybe "lawsuit" wasn't the first thing that came to a patient's or victim's mind out here when they were injured. I'm sure I would find out eventually how things worked and how people reacted in this town, but for today, I was definitely overthinking the situation. All over a sliding-glass door. But then maybe I was just too well-rested, and my mind was running wind sprints.

Granite Falls is near the junction of US Route 281, which spans the continental United States north to south from the Canadian border in North Dakota all the way down to the Mexican border in the Rio Grande Valley, and US Route 71, which runs in an east–west direction for a relatively short distance of 250 miles. It's in the Texas Hill Country, an area of Central and West Texas noted for . . . well, hills. The Hill Country contains twenty-five counties and the metropolitan areas of Austin and San Antonio. The geography is shaped by the dissolving of water-soluble rocks, especially granite and limestone. The topography is also influenced by the Llano Uplift, which includes the second-largest granite dome in the US.

These geological formations influenced the naming of counties and towns in the Hill Country many years ago: Limestone County, Granite Falls, Marble Falls, Highland Haven, and the town of Llano, to name a few. The Highland Lakes complex has also influenced the area, starting with a series of dams along the Colorado River, which created Lake Buchanan, Lake LBJ, Lake Marble Falls, Lake Travis, and Lake Austin. Horseshoe Bay, Cottonwood Shores, and Granite Shoals reflect naming tributes to various bodies of water created by the construction of the Granite Shoals Dam by the Lower Colorado River Authority in 1950.

All this geography and geology created over millions of years of planetary construction combined with the more-recent engineering by human hands and minds resulted in a spectacular blend of rolling hills and lakes, with a mild climate and relatively low humidity. Not to say it didn't get cold in the winter, and yes there was heat in the summer, but it was a spectacular place to live. Which is why I found myself at Hill Country Medical Center, sitting in the midst of all this Texas beauty.

There was a security desk adjacent to a wall in the middle of the entry corridor. I introduced myself to the guard sitting there. He referred to a clipboard and gave me a nod. "Dr. Brady, welcome to Hill Country Medical Center. Dr. Owens's office is down the hall to your left. Have a good day, sir."

I followed the hallway as instructed and said good morning to the receptionist at a semicircular desk adjacent to the administrative offices. "I'm Dr. Jim Bob Brady. I have an appointment with Dr. Owens?"

The nameplate at the desk she was occupying read Lucinda Williams. She stood, shook my hand, asked if I needed a beverage other than the coffee, water, and sodas that were set up in the conference room.

"That sounds fine to me. Is your mother a fan? Of Lucinda Williams?"

"Oh, yes, that's about all I heard growing up. Country, blues, rock, and folk all rolled into one strong husky voice. Just call me Lucy, please."

She was medium height, trim, cute but not pretty in a women's magazine sort of way. Her brown hair was trimmed in sort of a pixie style. She had on what I would call a nurses' scrub uniform with loose-fitting pants and pullover top, all in blue. What I noticed most was a left black eye. She seemed to have a look of melancholy about her. Why I thought that, I'm not sure. I had a myriad of patients over the years with all sorts of orthopedic problems, but I could never isolate those problems away from personality issues in my clientele. I could spot a depressed patient, that's for certain.

"How's the other fellow?" I asked.

"Excuse me?"

"The black eye."

"Oh, that. I was squatting down at home, trying to retrieve a chafing dish from under the counter, and slammed my forehead on the edge of a cabinet door. The doctors x-rayed it, said nothing was broken and my eye wasn't damaged. It doesn't really hurt any longer; now it's just the subject of conversation."

She changed that subject quickly and said, "Let me show you the conference room, Dr. Brady. I also function as Dr. Owens's administrative assistant, so if you are in need of something, please let me know."

The interior of the facility was beautiful, with walls of white limestone, plentiful in the Hill Country of Texas. The floors were of a matching color in some sort of durable ceramic tile. The ceiling was very high, with fans rotating slowly. There was a time when fans were not allowed in clinical areas due to the supposed risk of increased infections, but that had been debunked. In warm climates and summer seasons, fans were essential for adequate ventilation.

I noticed signs for Radiology, MRI and CT Scanning, Laboratory, Emergency Room, Urgent Care Center, and Outpatient Chemotherapy. The building had three stories, and I assumed for the moment that the operating rooms, recovery rooms, and ICUs were on the second floor. The third floor was more than likely hospital beds and nursing stations. Having been working in twenty-five- to thirty-story buildings for most of my training and career, this facility seemed to have all the right divisions, just on a much smaller scale.

Lucy escorted me into a conference room with a mahogany table surrounded by eight comfortable chairs with a purple print pattern on the seats and backs. The fellow at the head of the table stood and introduced himself.

"I'm Buck Owens, Dr. Brady. Pleasure to meet you. Welcome to HCMC."

He was somewhat shorter than me, with a tanned and lined face and a full head of gray hair.

"Please, call me Jim or Jim Bob. Seems I am in the presence of music royalty today. A Buck Owens and a Lucinda Williams."

He laughed. "My given name is Royal Owens, Royal having been my mother's maiden name. I'm a little older than you, but you may remember that naming children in the old days was about making a tribute to relatives long passed or creating nicknames that ascribed certain traits of an individual."

"Oh yes, I had eight aunts and uncles on my dad's side, and another eight on my mother's side, and each and every one had a given name and a nickname. With their spouses, that made thirty-two different names to remember at the family reunions. And the names weren't easy, they were like Tinkum for Lyla, and Dude for Gladys, and Girlie for Margaret. Bizarre stuff. I finally gave up and just called my older relatives ma'am and sir."

"So you can understand why I finally had folks call me Buck. A name like 'Royal' got your butt kicked when I was growing up in Weatherford, Texas, but 'Buck' got me a free pass. At any rate, I'm happy to have you here today. You'll meet some other folks a little later. Tell me a little about yourself, if you don't mind. I obviously have your bio here, but I'd like to hear you tell your story in your own words."

"I grew up in West Texas and Waco, went to Baylor undergraduate school. Go Bears! Then I went down to Houston, graduated from Baylor Med School, and did my internship and orthopedic surgery residency at the University Hospitals. After that training was done, I did a hip and knee replacement fellowship at Special Surgery in New York, then returned to Houston and joined the University Orthopedic Group, part of the University Hospital complex. I served as a clinician and a Professor of Orthopedic Surgery there for almost thirty years. Now I'm on a three-month sabbatical, sort of a retirement trial run, trying to find my niche in life. I have the option to return to my old job after the sabbatical, and after all this looking around I'm doing, maybe I'll do just that. But for now, I am actively seeking a new environment of some sort. And I'm not even sure what that is supposed to be. And it may not involve being an orthopedic surgeon any longer, although as far as I can tell, I have limited other skills."

"It's nice to have the luxury of finding yourself without having to worry about making a living at the same time. I understand you came into a . . . shall we say, financial windfall?"

"Yes. How in the world would you know about that?"

"Harold Sanders was an old friend of mine from the University of Texas days and the oil patch days. I've kept in touch with the family. I happened to be on the hunting trip when he was shot."

Mr. Harold Sanders was chairman of the University Hospital board and a prominent Houston citizen and oil wildcatter. He had been shot in the leg during opening weekend of spring turkey season many years prior by a colleague, and he eventually died of diabetic-related complications. In his will, he had left me 100 acres of land in Cotulla, in South Texas, which turned out to be chock full of oil and natural gas. After the final distribution some years later, his wife and sons bought me out of the property, and I ended up with over $16 million dollars free and clear of taxes and legal fees. That windfall had allowed me to reduce my work schedule at University Orthopedics, and it gave my wife Mary Louise and I the opportunity to travel and enjoy our free time, since the tax-free interest on that money was three times what I had been taking home after taxes and expenses as a surgeon working fifty to seventy hours per week.

"Wow, what a small world. But your 'oil patch days'? I thought you were an MD. Lucy introduced you as Dr. Owens."

"I was a family doc for many years, but I invested in the oil business through some old college buddies of mine, one of which was Harold Sanders. We got lucky on a few wells in the Permian Basin, which set me up for life. I eventually retired from patient care and found my calling in the hospital administration business. With some wealthy and generous benefactors, we established this medical center several years back. We have outlying clinics in Burnet, Llano, Brady, and Georgetown, and several more in the wings, all feeding patients down here. I've found that there are many other ways to treat patients and influence the course of an individual's health care besides being on the front lines of medicine. Of course, we need those patient-care doctors as well, but I was able to change directions in my life, much as it sounds like the situation you found yourself in. The biggest problem I had to overcome was the guilt."

"Guilt? About what, abandoning your training and direct patient care? I'm already losing sleep over it and I'm only one month into the sabbatical."

Buck laughed. "See, that insidious guilt has already crept in and found you. That's the way we docs are engineered, feeling that direct patient care is the only avenue to justify all that training. But I'm telling you, Jim Bob, there are many other ways to stay involved in medicine and help folks. You don't have to worry about forsaking the Hippocratic oath. You'll find your niche, just wait and see.

"In case you were wondering how I came into contact with you and asked you to come over and visit with us, it was through the Sanders family. They heard we were looking for another orthopedic surgeon with a hip and knee subspecialty, and although Mrs. Sanders had passed away some years back, the sons remembered you well. The family recommended you for consideration here at HCMC, thinking you might be interested in a change of scenery, now that you and your wife had become financially independent. One of Harold's sons serves on our board."

"That answers the question we had about the contact. It came unexpectedly through a headhunter, a firm that I had not even been in touch with. It seemed odd at the time, but since Mary Louise and I had leased an apartment on the water here at Horseshoe Bay Resort for a month, and we've been playing golf almost every day, we were obviously familiar with the area. We thought it mighty coincidental to hear about a potential job opportunity in an area where we were staying, and falling in love with, by the way."

"Where is your wife?"

"She's meeting me. I believe she had a date with the hair stylist. She should be here any moment."

"Then let's get that tour going, shall we?"

ABOUT THE AUTHOR

Dr. John Bishop has led a triple life. This orthopedic surgeon and keyboard musician has combined two of his talents into a third, as the author of the beloved Doc Brady mystery series. Beyond applying his medical expertise at a relatable and comprehensible level, Dr. Bishop, through his fictional counterpart Doc Brady, also infuses his books with his love of not only Houston and Galveston, Texas, but especially with his love for his adored wife. Bishop's talented Doc Brady is confident yet humble; brilliant, yet a genuinely nice and funny guy who happens to have a knack for solving medical mysteries. Above all, he is the doctor who will cure you of your blues and boredom. Step into his world with the first five books of the series, and you'll be clamoring for more.

Printed in Great Britain
by Amazon

16809179R00132